DIRTY DEEDS DONE
DIRT CHEAP

DIRTY DEEDS DONE DIRT CHEAP

PROTECTED BY THE DAMNED, BOOK 7

MICHAEL TODD   MICHAEL ANDERLE
LAURIE STARKEY

DISRUPTIVE IMAGINATION

Proprietor
Spurlock's - Henderson NV

Editor
Lynne Stiegler

DEDICATION

To Family, Friends and
Those Who Love
to Read.
May We All Enjoy Grace
to Live the Life We Are
Called.

— Michael Anderle

"Thank you everyone for joining the call." General Brushwood sat at a large oval table with his men. The mercenary team leads from around the country were on a screen in front of him. "After recent events, we found it important to get everyone together and on the same page. It's obvious there's been a change— an escalation of sorts— going on with the demons. We have all lost good men and women in this battle. I would like to start the meeting off by hearing from Amy."

From every angle the general considered, the government and the mercenaries were on track to work together a lot more often than either really wanted to.

Given the events so far, from the large incursions to the attacks on both Korbin's and Amy's teams, they *had* to pull together, because if something didn't change they were going to be burying a lot *more* comrades.

General Brushwood and other heads of state had wanted a face-to-face meeting, but with the mercenary teams not only bogged down by calls but short a lot of men there was no way any of them could get away long enough for a meeting like that.

Especially one that for some was clear across the country.

Due to the past relations between the government and the mercenary teams, the mercs pushed to do this thing *their* way.

However, setting up a secure conference call for teams across the United States was something even Derek couldn't have done safely yet. The general'd had his team set it up so they were sure the video feed would be completely secure from prying eyes.

No one wanted government representatives talking about demons on the six o'clock news.

Obviously this wasn't ideal for the government, but they had to meet the mercs in the middle or nothing would get done.

General Brushwood and the others knew it was an essential alliance, but they had to prove they were in it one hundred percent or the mercs would continue to work as they had for decades.

Hurting everyone in the process

The general continued, "For those from the military, Amy is the leader of Amy's Assassins. The team was just in an ambush that left one team member dead and several others injured. Amy?"

"Thank you, General," she said, shuffling her papers. "So, everyone now knows that we lost one of our best teammates and are tending to those injured. What you *don't* know is what happened that night."

Her voice changed. It was still strong, but with a hint of the pain the ambush caused. "It began as a normal call, and we headed out thinking it would be the usual human demon situation. However, about two thirds of the way through the fight the warehouse was ambushed by a group of humans with demon advantages. It was no longer just Damned fighting Damned. This was a tactical team, combat-trained and determined to take our team down. They had weapons and what looked to be a command structure.

"Immediately everything on the comms went to shit. We were shocked and there was a lot of chatter. We had seen fighting demons before—even those still in full human bodies—but never *militarized* ones. It was both concerning and confusing."

"Did they talk to one another?" someone yelled.

"Did they have uniforms? Were they using any unusual weapons?" another person asked.

"Who was their leader?"

This was a new dawn in the age of fighting demons; something that no one had expected. The ones they fought before had been rogues, and if they had banded together it was for their own purposes. They definitely hadn't been trained like those Amy said had attacked the mercenaries.

Amy shook her head and tried to answer what questions she could.

"We couldn't tell if they were communicating verbally, but they did use tactical hand signals," Amy told the group. "They were dressed in black and used street weapons, but nothing specialized. As far as the leader, he didn't seem to be the mastermind. He was more like an officer leading his troops into battle. Look, I know everyone has a million questions—and so do we—but with one dead and three still in the hospital, details are still a little scarce. We can't talk to the injured right now—not securely—to find out what they saw. We've been over the operation with the remaining team members repeatedly, though."

"Thank you, Amy," the general said, raising his voice above the babble of conversation. Everyone quieted almost instantly. "I know you have a lot of questions, and so do we. The government began an investigation into the ambush of Amy's team immediately after we got word. On surveillance video we traced the attackers from the outskirts of the town to the warehouse and back, but unfortunately their vehicles had been reported as stolen. We attempted to follow, but they disappeared into the brush. As of this moment we have not figured out where exactly they went."

"They couldn't have just disappeared," someone said.

"No, they couldn't," the general replied, flipping a sheet in his notes. "These are real survivalists; there is no doubt about that. They have probably been off the grid for years somewhere right here in the United States. We neither know where they are currently, nor where they have been for the last decade. This meeting has been called because I need you to understand—and I can't stress this enough— the importance of cooperation between the military and the mercenaries."

There were a couple of grunts and William Hunt out of Texas spoke up. "What about the last century, during which cooperation has been nothing but a joke?"

"Bill, we are remedying that as well as we can," General

Brushwood stated flatly. "We all need to come together to find these people. They are both the military's and the mercenaries' primary target, since they pose a significant risk to the health and safety of us all. If we don't come together there might not be anyone left to…"

"…left to rally behind. We are constantly searching for additional intel, and as soon as we know more we will share it with you. We would appreciate it if you did the same. Thank you all for joining us, and everyone has my direct number for contact," the general finished.

The video ended, the chatter cutting off. Korbin, Calvin, and Katie looked over their laptops at each other and Calvin's eyebrow arched. They shut their computers in unison and sat in silence thinking about what had just been said.

"That *is* concerning," Katie said. "But I think this is a good thing—a push toward finding the control center so we can shut it down."

"I agree," Korbin replied. "But it's also dangerous, which is why I'm glad we moved to this location. I feel more secure here, and we have the technology to do so much more."

" It's pretty sweet with the tunnel system. Like covert ops." Calvin chuckled.

"With Vogue-level décor." Katie winked.

"That was all Stephanie." Korbin shrugged. "Not that I'm complaining! I really like the shower heads."

"And the new mattresses," Katie pointed out.

"And the new weapons locker," Calvin added, rubbing his palms together. "It's a beautiful room of destruction just waiting for the day it will be used."

Katie leaned toward Calvin. "You have a war complex," she teased, standing up. "But we love you anyway."

"We all do." He chuckled again as he stood.

The phone rang as he and Katie started for the door and they stopped. Korbin groaned and picked up the phone.

His answer was short. "This is Korbin."

"It's Brushwood," the voice stated loudly enough for Katie to hear. "I wanted to find out if you and some of your team could meet us at Nellis in three hours?"

"Of course, General," Korbin replied, looking at and Katie and Calvin. "Do we need full armor and weapons?"

"Better bring something just in case, but don't go overboard. We will see you there."

"Right," Korbin said. "Three hours."

Korbin hung up and rubbed his face, then looked at the other two.

Katie shook her head. "He is determined to work us to death, I think."

"He wants me and a small team to meet him at Nellis," Korbin told them. "So I suppose we suit up and hit the helicopter. It's not far, so take the time to make sure you have everything you need. I have no idea what we will be walking into."

"Just us three?" Calvin asked. "With Derek gone we are shorthanded."

For a moment Katie's chest ached from the loss of her

teammate as she thought about him taking his last breath on that battlefield.

She hated that he had died, and she hated the feeling of grief. It made her want to kick ass even more.

"I know," Korbin said. "I'm not really sure what to do about that just yet. All the teams are hurting, that's for sure. Amy is short four people right now, and has no idea when the three in the hospital will be back. The six of us may have to deal with everything for the time being. I have a feeling anyone brought on will go to Amy's team until she has the numbers she needs. Needs must when the devil drives."

"Right." Calvin nodded. "Katie and I will get suited up… and we'll grab some extra gear just in case. Is there anything specific I can bring you from the locker?"

"No," Korbin replied. "I have my weapons in the office, but thank you. Hopefully this isn't about a fight."

"All right, boss." Katie tapped the back of her former chair. "We'll see you in a few. And don't let the stress get you. We need clear heads, whether this is a meeting or a fight. These aren't our people."

Korbin nodded, and Calvin and Katie walked out of the office to gear up.

They headed to the training area in silence, and Calvin split off to the armory while Katie put on her normal gear. The meeting concerned her more than she let on. She figured the changes in attacks were T'Chezz's doing.

I don't know, Pandora said doubtfully.

You don't know what? That your brother is a psycho? Are you getting soft on me?

Yeah, right, bitch. Pandora scowled. *I just mean this sounds*

7

more like Moloch getting his greasy little fingers in the pie, not my brother.

Who is Moloch? Katie almost didn't want to ask the question.

He's a high-level demon, top eight to be exact, and extremely powerful, Pandora stated. *Not only that, but he is smart as hell. He does more thinking before he finishes breakfast in the morning than T'Chezz does all week.*

Great, Katie griped, and shoved her knives into the sheaths of her vest. *Just what we need...someone even more powerful than your idiot brother. I'm gonna need to buy a tank to knock him back to hell.*

Maybe, Pandora agreed seriously. *But all I know is, if this is true... If it's Moloch behind this, it's not good. In fact, I would say the situation went from bad to dire in about three seconds.*

Katie wasn't too keen on Pandora's final comment.

Moloch is no one to fuck with.

"You think it's an incursion call?" Stephanie asked Damian. She was watching Calvin walk toward the training center.

"No," Damian replied. "I mean, I could be wrong, but it's probably a follow-up meeting after the conference call they had earlier."

"I forgot about that call," Stephanie muttered. "Whatever is going on, though, it's obvious that it's getting crazy out there. Things aren't like what I thought they would be."

"Having second thoughts?" Damian asked, one eyebrow raised.

"No." She waved a hand. "Just learning the ropes and reality, that's all."

He looked around for his drink. "Truth is, things *are* different," Damian told her, grabbing his coffee from his desk and taking a sip. The aroma reminded him of the good things in life; things that were worth saving.

"It's been a lot more intense lately, almost out of control. Not that it was simple before, but it wasn't anything like this."

"Yet here we are." Stephanie sipped her brew. "And now we have to figure out where to go next. Things kind of took a serious turn with the attack on Amy's Assassins. I feel like everyone is running around like chickens with their heads cut off."

"We are," Damian sighed. "But the important thing to figure out is where we go from here. It won't do us any good to focus on the others until we have control over our situation. I know Korbin wants to help everyone, but that will be impossible unless we can function on our own."

"So what's our first step?" Stephanie asked.

"Well, first and foremost, not to diss Derek's memory, but we desperately need an IT guy. They are the foundation of our operations. They give us intel for future incursions and a map of the issues in the area. We use that for black ops, spy work, and almost everything else. Unfortunately, none of us who are left have any clue how to work all that stuff. Korbin knows more than us, but he can't run it full-time. He's the leader. We need to find someone who can tackle it like Derek could."

"Either someone Damned or willing to work with us for life." Stephanie shook her head. "That's a needle-in-ahaystack kind of person. What about New York? They have a double-sized team. Can they spare someone?"

"No," Damian replied. "They have a double-sized team with a triple-sized threat area. They can barely afford for one of their team to go to the bathroom, much less come out here to help us. What about you? You seem to know a lot of people, and you have contacts everywhere."

"Yeah, but most of those people are manual-labor or illegal-activity contacts." Stephanie shrugged. "Or the occasional businessmen or women who want an outlet, who will speak the right words, or moan at appropriate times. Even on the mile-long list of names I have, finding someone that fits the bill for what we need might be impossible."

"We'll need to keep our eyes peeled, then." Damian looked around before running a hand through his hair. "Intel is almost more important than the battle itself. With the demons hunting us at every turn like lions stalking prey, we could find ourselves backed right into a bloody corner."

2

C alvin tossed his bags into the back of the helicopter and climbed in, closing the door and nodding to the pilot as he put on his headset. He buckled in and looked at Katie.

She was fiddling with the bag of chips in her hand and smirked. "What? I'm hungry."

"Did you ask Dad if we can eat in his multi-million-dollar bird?"

Katie looked at Korbin with a chip halfway to her mouth. "Dad?"

He ignored her as she tossed the chip into her mouth. "You guys ready?" Korbin asked, shaking his head.

"Sure thing, boss," Calvin replied. "Not flying us today?"

"Not quite done with my lessons. I figured, unless it's an emergency, I won't risk your lives."

"We appreciate that." Katie tossed another chip into her mouth.

"Okay, so I haven't had a chance to watch the show lately. What's been going on?" Korbin asked.

"Oh my God!" Katie shouted, a tiny piece of chip flying out to hit Calvin on the cheek. "Oh my God, I'm so sorry!" She reached over to brush the speck off Calvin's cheek. He shook his head as Katie turned to Korbin in excitement. "There was a portal to hell in the last one. All I kept thinking about was whether they would find my car."

"Of course, they didn't," Calvin interjected. "But Luther found out that Esmond, the new 'chauffeur' for the richie-rich white folks, is actually a hell-demon…or so they call them."

"Slightly redundant, don't you think?" Korbin rolled his eyes.

"Yeah, but these people don't know they're real," Katie replied earnestly. "Besides, they are just trying to come up with something inventive. They don't realize that they're surrounded by it all day long."

"Their producer is probably a demon." Calvin smiled and looked out the window. There was a house fire below. "Damn, you don't think that has anything to do with—"

"No," Korbin interjected. "Probably just someone who forgot to turn off the iron. I know our world is nothing but demons, but these people have no clue."

"True," Calvin replied, turning back to Katie.

Korbin wanted the conversation to stay on the soaps. He wanted them distracted from the news of the conference call long enough to calm the nerves that he knew they felt.

The sudden news of a hell-demon "Damned" group was

shocking even to him, and he had seen a lot of shit in his day.

On top of that was the new alliance between the military and the mercenaries, something that was more than a touchy subject. If a team member hadn't been around for the past dramas they had *definitely* been told about them, and it had created an animosity that Korbin feared wouldn't be squashed just because—in the face of a new type of demon—everyone wanted to begin to cooperate.

"I think this is all a good thing." Calvin eyed Katie to check that she wasn't going to spit any more chips at him. "Maybe with the military on our side we will get a little more support. I mean, think about the compound battle forever ago—what would have happened if we'd had a couple badass helicopters there."

"Ok, I can see that." Korbin pursed his lips. "And I have to admit, Katie might have helped by reaching out to the military when she did. Otherwise we might still be separated by the past, and we definitely need their intel right now."

"And you were worried." Katie scoffed. "I *told* you it would be a good thing. One of these days you are going to trust me."

"I wouldn't have allowed you to go if I didn't trust you," Korbin replied. "It's *them* I don't trust."

Calvin spoke up. "Well, we will all have to learn to try… for right now, anyway."

"Do you have any idea how long it will take Joshua to create more rounds?" Korbin asked. " We are going through them like water and you gave two cases to the general, who we all know will be wanting more very soon."

"Right now we have another two hundred," Katie answered. "But if we have more situations like this, we are going to have to come up with some sort of a deal to have someone else use our metal and build the rounds themselves. It's one thing for Joshua to create the metal, it's a whole other thing to hand-make these bullets. He is struggling to do that and continue to make weapons—he's working nineteen hours a day. I can't ask him to work anymore. In fact, I think he needs some rest."

Korbin nodded. He didn't like that solution one bit—allowing someone from the outside anywhere near their precious metal.

He wasn't sure there was anyone he could trust who wouldn't ask questions or become curious. They couldn't allow it to get into the hands of the wrong people; it might devastate their efforts, and they certainly didn't need their own weapons used against them.

Which was the bigger risk.

"Let's hope it doesn't come to that," Korbin replied finally. "I'm still not happy putting the military on our 'friends' list. I don't need them to turn on us when they think they don't need us anymore."

"It's a risk, sure," Katie agreed. "But right now the alternative leaves us six feet under."

Damian sat in the pew in his sanctuary quietly contemplating the past few weeks.

There had been such a change in the way the demons were fighting; the way they banded together, their size, and their resilience. It was reminiscent of the passages he often read in the Bible of the end of days.

He knew there was a bigger fight brewing, and he was concerned that even someone as capable and powerful as Katie wouldn't be able to withstand what was coming.

He felt the need to do something about it, not to just sit back and wait for another attack.

He looked around. There was no intel coming from their base due to Derek's death, but that didn't mean they couldn't be proactive.

He stood and left the sanctuary, pulling out his cell phone as he took the elevator to ground level. Cell service in the tunnels was spotty, and he needed a breath of fresh air anyway.

Once he had gone outside, he scrolled through his numbers to find Father Avery's contact information. He was the priest he and Katie had found half dead in the small church during one of their more brutal incursions. He dialed the number and pulled the phone to his ear.

"Damian," the priest answered in a jolly tone. "It's so good to hear from you."

"You too, Father, I apologize for not calling sooner, but I wanted you to get rest and get better."

"It's all right. The sisters at the hospital told me you called every day to check on me," he replied.

"How have you been doing since then?"

"I've had to make amends for the horrible situation that unfurled, to both the church and to God," Avery stated. "The guilt has burned inside me every day. Probably the other priests are tired of my sulking. Fortunately, though, I am back to serving God and the congregation. Regrettably, the other priest—the one who had the demon in the first place—was excommunicated. There was nothing we could do. It riddled many here with guilt for not seeing the signs."

"You shouldn't put that on your shoulders," Damian replied. "God was there, and while you may not have seen his signs, you were distracted because you were helping others. That can be forgiven, I promise you. Sometimes we do the work of twenty men, but we are *still* only mortal."

"That is the truth," Father Avery replied. "What can I help you with today?"

"I was wondering if the church had any intel regarding the new strategies the demons are using?" Damian asked. "There have been some alarming attacks; things that make us think an uprising may be on the horizon."

The phone was silent long enough that Damian considered asking if he was still there.

"That is very distressing indeed," Father Avery finally replied. "But no, I have not heard anything of the sort in recent meetings. That, of course, doesn't mean the church isn't aware of anything, but they may not be disseminating the information to *us*. I will look into it. I have some friends higher up on the food chain who may be able to shine some light on the subject. Is it bad?"

"There was an organized attack about a week or so ago that left one dead and three in critical care," Damian responded. "They were said to have been almost like us, only fighting the opposite side."

"Damned?"

"Yes, a group of humans damned *just* like us," Damian

replied. " It could have been completely random, but with our losses here we are currently struggling to get any intel."

"I'm sorry for all the lives lost. We will say a prayer."

"Thank you," Damian said, letting out a deep breath. "The tides seem to be shifting."

"They always do," the other priest replied. "Throughout history, they have ebbed and flowed. Sometimes the current is strong and sucks us under, and other times it is a beautiful swim."

"Very nicely put." Damian smiled. "Other than that, how is the church? How are the others after the battle there?"

"We are still rebuilding, and we lost a lot of precious old historical items, but they are just things. We can move on without them. As far as the people, the press has slowed down, though there is still talk of the 'rogue shooter' they have pinned it all on. I feel bad about the lies, but I know it is in the best interests of the community. I just hope God agrees with that when I reach the Pearly Gates."

"A man like you should never question that," Damian stated firmly.

"Thank you. And how are things with you?"

"They are okay. Just settling into a new place and getting my sanctuary set up," Damian replied. "No one attends here, and I have put my other outreach projects on hold while we are going through all of this. Still, I find peace there, and I do what I can for the others. Sometimes it feels like I'm alone, but when I remember where I came from and how I got here, I feel that I am where I'm supposed to be."

"You certainly are," the other priest said. "You are *always* where you are supposed to be, even if you can't see it at the time. Things can get stressful, I know, but remember your vows and remember your purpose. There is no one better suited for the job."

"I appreciate those words, and I won't keep you," Damian said. "Thank you for taking my call."

"Any time, Damian, and I will get back to you with that information as soon as I hear," Father Avery responded.

"Thank you, Father," Damian replied and pressed End.

He stood there for a moment and thought about the scene that day at the church, and a shiver went down his spine.

He feared it wouldn't be the last time he would see something like that.

The staff stood back from the helicopter pads as two helos began to land. On the right was Korbin's Eurocopter X3, sleek, white, fast, and on the left was the military Black Hawk. Normally the Black Hawk would have been a sight to see—a vehicle of precision with excellent fighting ability —but next to the Eurocopter it looked like a giant piece of heavy metal.

"I feel like the general is checking his package right now." One of the airmen chuckled.

"And finding himself at a loss." Another outright laughed. "If I were the general, I might just order a takeover of the X3 so I wouldn't feel like I had to compete with something like that."

"Nah," the first replied. "My junk is big enough to compensate. I'd just stand up straight and laugh at the expensive, beautifully designed, makes-me-want-to-weep Eurocopter."

"Ha-ha. Sounds like you have a case of chopper envy, my friend."

"Or penis envy," the third airman said with a smirk. "I, on the other hand, have neither. Mine is so big they'd need both those choppers to get me off the ground."

"That's not what Jennings said after your last date." The first airman laughed.

"Nah," the second guy said, ignoring the banter. "The Black Hawk is superior in so many ways. It's meant for combat. It's heavier, so you can mount way better weapons, and it won't go down from a little gunfire. The X3, you put a turret on there and that bitch is going down from the weight."

Just then Katie stepped out of the X3 with a look of determination on her face and her hair blowing wildly in the wind. Her outfit was skintight as always, and her breasts looked to be larger.

All three of the airmen's jaws dropped and the second guy began to chuckle.

"Okay, there is no fucking way you're going to find such a hot babe coming out of a Black Hawk. That's it… your copter wins hands down."

"I wonder if that comes standard when you buy one, because if so, take my fucking money," the third guy said. "She can hold my Johnson in her lap."

The first snickered. "If she has tweezers."

Katie looked down at her boots, noticing the scuffs on the toe. She had forgotten to clean them after the last fight, but she didn't care. She was just headed to a meeting. If they didn't like her boots they could suck it.

I'm sure one of those hot little numbers would like you to suck it, Pandora cooed.

Katie flicked her eyes to the three airmen talking on the sidelines.

Mmmm, that tall one is pretty scrumptious, Katie replied.

All three are pretty scrumptious with those tight uniforms, big muscles, and good-boy smiles, Pandora purred. *I'd take all three of them at once if I had it my way.*

Good thing you don't, Katie mumbled as she followed Calvin and Korbin toward the general.

The general stood next to Colonel Jehovivich and two men wearing black suits, black glasses, and black ties.

Katie lifted an eyebrow at the two men, wondering when the aliens had attacked, but didn't comment. She figured they wouldn't get the "Men in Black" reference anyway; the sticks were too far up there.

She followed them through the base and into a secure room set up with keypads, eye scanners, and the lot. Apparently what they were about to discuss was anything but casual.

3

D amian returned to the chapel to think about his call and reflect on the things the priest had discussed with him.

He'd never felt right for his current position, but no matter how unusual a religious figure he was, his path had always been in God's hands. He still needed to find a balance, although that was something he'd been trying for since becoming Damned.

"Damian," Stephanie called over the base's intercom. "There is a potential possession going on in North Las Vegas."

Damian looked at the neon cross on the wall and smiled, then stood and pressed the intercom button.

"Who made the call?"

"The Ghost Hunters?" she said, unsure. "They said they know you."

"Yeah," Damian replied with a sigh. "I had a call with

them a few months back; one of Katie's first. I'll be over in just a second."

Damian thought about that possession as he headed out: how Katie had taken down a giant demon, they'd seen walls that bled, and that the ghost hunters had been infected on the scene.

It had definitely *not* been the most fun possession call he'd ever had. He could peg that callout as the beginning of all the crazy shit.

He walked into the office and nodded at Stephanie. "I'm going to take Eric with me as backup. Can you call him?"

"Right here, dude," Eric said, walking around the corner. "I heard the call over the speakers."

"Good." Damian strode toward the door, waving a hand over his shoulder. "Stephanie, you hold down the fort. Eric, let's go."

"You got it," Stephanie agreed as Eric and Damian headed toward the armory.

Eric caught up with Damian. "So, is it my turn for a 'date' like the one you took Katie on?" He laughed. "She mentions it from time to time, so I fully expect the same good time."

"Right," Damian grumped, walking into the armory. He shoved a pistol into Eric's hand. "Suit up."

"You have to promise to be gentle with me." Eric waggled his eyebrows and chuckled as he put on his gear. "This is my first time. Of course, if this is the kind of date I've heard about, I know I'm in the best hands."

Damian ignored him as they headed toward the elevator. They rode it to ground level and went over to the garage. Damian got in the driver's seat and waited for Eric to climb into the passenger side.

"Buckle up," Damian ordered, putting the car in drive and pulling quickly onto the road that led to the gate.

"You *are* in a hurry." Eric smiled. "I'm offended that you didn't buy me flowers first."

Damian stopped at the gate and glanced at Eric, who was chuckling to himself.

"You can hope it's *not* like that date," Damian grumbled. "Since if it's just you and me and *that* happens again? We will both probably be dead."

Damian hit the gas and they surged through the open gate toward the highway. Eric's smile slowly faded and he cleared his throat, suddenly looking nervous.

Damian smirked slightly, thankful that his teammate had finally shut up.

Once through the scanners and outside security checks, Katie, Korbin, and Calvin followed the general, the colonel, and the two men in black into the interior of a building where the four military officials walked straight through the metal detector.

Korbin stepped forward and froze when the buzzers and sirens went off around him. He chuckled and stepped back. General Brushwood simply raised an eyebrow.

Korbin laughed as he pulled his pistols out of their holsters and handed them over to the guard.

He then removed a short sword from the sheath on his back, and about fifty-seven cents' worth of change from his pocket. Katie giggled as the guard looked down at the change and waved a wand over Korbin.

He was clear and proceeded through the detector. He stopped beside the general as Calvin stepped forward with a not-so-very happy look on his face. None of them liked to be unarmed, that was for damn sure, but Calvin knew not to make a fuss.

Calvin handed over his pistol and held the knife just out of the soldier's reach.

His voice was firm. "I want *this* knife back. Not any other knife, but *this* knife." He stared at the guard.

The guard nodded and Calvin handed him the knife, straightened his shirt indignantly, and walked through the metal detector. Apparently, Calvin didn't carry change in his pocket like Korbin did.

They all looked at Katie, who stood there staring at them. Korbin immediately let out a sigh, knowing exactly what was going to happen.

The rest of them just assumed she was going to hand over her weapons and the guard reached toward her, but she slapped his hand away with an irritated red glare. Slowly she turned to the group on the far side of the alarm.

She eyed them all. "Now, why the fuck would *any* of you think for one second I am going to give up my weapons?"

Calvin covered his mouth to stifle his laugh.

He snorted instead, and the colonel threw him an irritated glance.

Calvin knew Katie wasn't going to fall for that shit, and she was pretty much the only one who could make a scene without starting an argument. The general stood quietly for a moment, then stepped forward.

"This is a military facility." He eyed her calmly. "We have weapons regulations, or to say it another way, we *all* give up our weapons to ensure safety throughout the entire base. It is not just for you, it's for everyone—including me."

"Riiight." Katie smiled. "But suppose I have weapons that I can't physically leave behind...something much more dangerous than my knives?"

The general tilted his head and lifted an eyebrow, not exactly sure what she meant. He had seen her in action, sure, but his mind ran down a list of weapons she could possibly be talking about.

Finally she sighed and shook her head. "Okay, do we have any volunteers?"

Calvin looked at the assembled military types, who all wore looks of uncertainty mixed with a tiny bit of fear, smiles plastered on their faces. His eyes fell on Korbin, who shrugged and shook his head.

"All right, bitches, I'll be the damned volunteer of death." Calvin chuckled. "Seriously, I thought you folks were fearless. What the hell happened to that? You'll face down Vietnam, but you won't walk over to this lovely lady?"

"Right." Korbin scoffed under his breath.

Calvin sauntered back through the metal detector and winked at Katie. "Okay, honey, what are you going to show us? I bruise easily, though, so go easy on me unless it's one of *those* nights. But I've got to tell you in advance that I didn't bring any rope."

Katie rolled her eyes.

I like him, Pandora growled. *Can I play with him?*

Ewww, no! Because that would be like me playing with my brother in ways that just aren't right.

He's not your brother, in case you couldn't tell. Calvin's scrumptious dark meat and Korbin is a white breast...Damn, now I want chicken nuggets.

I'll remember that some other time. Remember, you aren't my sister, but that's how I think about you, Katie replied.

Pandora went quiet.

Katie grabbed Calvin's shoulders and turned him around next to her. He stood straight and looked at the general, who watched with curiosity.

The guard by the metal detector looked nervous and kept one hand on the butt of his pistol. Katie cleared her throat, lifted her hand to Calvin's face, and put one finger on his cheek.

Everybody froze for a second. They didn't understand what she was doing, but when her finger went from perfect and pretty to a two-inch demon claw they all took a step back, leaving Korbin in front of them.

He just rubbed his chin and chuckled.

"Does anyone believe he's going to take away *all* our weapons?" she asked. "You might as well give everybody weapons if you want them on an even footing while there are Damned in the house." She looked around. "Not a threat, just an observation."

Calvin looked down. "What, did I pee? I don't *feel* anything warm." He looked at the closest guard. "Hey, not trying to get weird, but there isn't a wet spot, is there?" The guard's eyes flicked down, then up to Calvin's face and he shook his head. "Oh, thank God!"

Colonel Jehovivich clenched her fists. She was angry as hell and stepped forward and opened her mouth to protest. The general put his hand up to stop the words and stepped up next to Korbin.

He lifted one eyebrow and smiled as he shook his head.

He could argue with her all day, but when it came down to it she was absolutely right. The rules hadn't been made with the Damned in mind, and anytime the humans were unarmed—no matter what actual weapons the infected were or were not carrying—they were at a disadvantage.

"At least she's honest," the general said to Korbin, then looked at Katie. "All right, bring your weapons. I don't care. I either trust you…"

He turned but looked back over his shoulder. "Or I *don't.*"

The others looked at the general, then at Katie, then back at the general before following him down the hall. Calvin patted her on the arm and followed Korbin. Katie smiled, feeling as if she had finally won one small battle. When she walked through security the alarms went off, but the guards waved her through…although they stood back slightly.

"Go on, go on," they griped. "It's not like we didn't *expect* that to happen."

After the group left, one leaned toward the other. "Did you happen to get a look at her hot…*weapons?*"

The other guard looked down. "I don't have a wet spot, do I?"

Eric looked out the window as they drove through a nice neighborhood in the north section of Las Vegas.

The houses were big, and the neighborhood didn't look to be any older than maybe three years. The trees were still pretty small, and most of the front yards were xeriscaped.

Eric was pretty shocked that they were in such a nice place. He had expected to go to the rough side of town, or maybe one of the poorer neighborhoods. Then again, he had heard all the stories from Stephanie and Katie about demons taking over the rich, so maybe this was the same kind of case.

When they pulled up in front of the house Eric whistled.

It looked like something out of a magazine. Everything was perfectly placed, from the hidden trashcans to the birdbath strategically centered in a precisely planted and manicured row of flowering bushes. He got out of the SUV and stood next to Damian, who pulled out his bible and holy water. "Where do they get the water?"

Eric smiled. "Wrong water."

Damian smirked but otherwise ignored his banter as Eric continued, "What we have here on our tour of the rich and famous is the perfect family home," he announced in a news-caster's voice. "This two-story four to five-bedroom house has perfect siding, a brand-new roof, and grass never touched by human feet because from what I can tell it's AstroTurf. The home is perfect for your two-and-a-half children, dog named Spot, and your husband wearing a BBQ Dad apron." He looked around, "I wonder if it comes with a trophy wife?"

Damian groaned, shot him an annoyed look, and

pushed a bag of gear into his chest. Eric grunted and chuckled as he followed the priest to the front door.

The three ghost hunters from the possession with Katie opened the door. The main guy stuck out his hand, but Damian just raised an eyebrow, then pulled out his light and flashed it into everyone's eyes.

He wasn't messing around with them this time, and would not go in if they had been possessed again.

"Relax." The leader laughed. "We aren't possessed this time. We actually took a minute before you came to double-check each other. You know, just to make sure we weren't going to trap you again."

"I appreciate that," Damian said quietly. "All right, so what do we have going on today?"

The leader stood to the side as Damian and Eric walked into the house. "Well, we have a teenage girl—parents called us earlier—who has been acting very strange since she got back from another girl's pajama party Saturday night."

"Great, a gaggle of teenage girls! What could possibly go wrong?" Damian groaned.

"Yeah." The leader scoffed. "These girls could have summoned any sort of nonsense by looking up some funny spell on the internet."

Eric spoke in a spooky voice. "Maybe they are obsessed with the dark side."

Damian shot him a glare and he immediately shut up, glancing around the room awkwardly. As they begin to climb the stairs they all stopped, feeling about a ten-degree drop in temperature.

Eric zipped up his jacket and looked at Damian. "That's not scary or anything," he whispered.

"That's right!" the ghost hunter to the left exclaimed. "We've got the real deal this time." He nodded in excitement. "There is *no* questioning that."

Eric looked at him funny, not sure why anyone would be so happy to be messing around with dark spirits. Then again, these guys had probably been doing this for years and rarely got even a *glimpse* of anything truly connected to spirits.

"Why are you looking at me like that?" The guy stared at Eric. "This the real thing here, and now we just need to get proof."

"We should already have proof," the second hunter said, rolling her eyes. "Of course, the *last* time we had something this certain somebody came along and destroyed all the evidence before we collected it. Maybe you could stay away from the videos this time, Damian?"

"Can't make any promises," Damian replied as he opened the door to the girl's room. "How old is she?"

"Fifteen, I think," the leader told him as he walked in carefully beside him.

The room was a typical teenager's, with posters, old stuffed animals, makeup, and clothes everywhere, and pictures of her and her friends in the mirror frame. Eric shook his head as he walked over to a pile of clothes by the closet, then tripped and fell into Damian's back.

He straightened, shaking his head. "Sorry, I—"

Damian put his finger to his lips and looked at the girl. Lying on the bed was a young woman of around fifteen, curled into a ball. She was drooling, her eyes were bloodshot, and her hair was frizzy and wild.

Eric swallowed hard and shook his head.

"*Quomodo audes huc venisti* fucking *adici debent. Et deprecari in oculis tuis caput et ex illis manducare prandium,*" the girl intoned in a deep and malevolent voice.

"What did she say?" Eric asked, his voice quivering.

"Oh, you know, the usual," Damian replied, opening his bible. "How she wants to eat my eyeballs for breakfast." Damian smiled but swallowed his joke. *Lord forgive me.* "Or your balls, I get *audes huc* mixed up sometimes."

"Oh," Eric squeaked. "I have to say, that is fucking terrifying."

4

K atie looked around the base hallway as she followed the others into a large room.

Gray; lots and lots of gray paint. How about sprucing it up with white every once in a while?

Where are the tittie posters? Pandora asked.

I think they went out with the last generation—or they hide them when demon-possessed women get near.

Why? Pandora asked. *I'm good with women being naked. Hell, I have to check out the competition. Sometimes they trip me up...like, I've noticed everyone is shaving down there. What's up with that? Are guys turned on by young stuff?*

They probably just don't want you to figure out what turns them on.

Oh... Yeah, I get that. Although, I have to say this one girl I saw had shaved an inverted triangle that pointed down. Considering some of the class-one idiots I've done in the past, that was a genius move. If they can't follow directions as clear as that, it's probably better you leave sooner rather than later. Especially if you think there isn't enough lube in...

NO! Katie yelled. *Please, for the love of—*

NO! Pandora interrupted quickly and vociferously. *You don't say* his *name and I won't say "anal sex."*

OH MY GOD! Katie shrieked.

YOU JUST SAID HIS NAME!

You said "anal sex" first! Katie argued.

I did not! Pandora argued, then settled down. *I just... Oh, fuck, I did. Okay, can we call a truce for now?*

Okay, truce for now. Let me get through this meeting, okay?

Mmmhmmm, Pandora replied.

Katie wasn't sure if that was agreement or just good enough for now, but she walked into the meeting room.

She shut the door behind them and went to the large round table, which had twenty chairs around it.

The seven of them took seats: Korbin, Calvin, and Katie on one side, the military four facing them.

There was silence for a few moments and the two men in suits just sat there. Finally they took off their sunglasses, but their stares were no better.

Katie put her hands on the table and twiddled her thumbs, pursed her lips, and looked at the large projection screen to the right of them.

She assumed that the video chat had been done in a similar room located wherever Brushwood had been at that moment.

She absolutely hated the idea of being a suit, forced to sit around tables like this all the time and listen to stuffed-shirt politicians bitch about their pockets while swindling the rest of the country out of what little they had left.

Being Damned didn't seem so bad compared to that.

After a few moments, though, she became restless. She sighed and looked at the general and the suited men.

"Okay," she said, slapping her hands on the table. "Have we finished the dick-measuring yet? Because if not, I gotta say," she quipped, "I can't compete."

Calvin started to snicker but broke it off when Korbin snapped his head around and gave him stink-eye.

He looked at Katie as well but she just shrugged her shoulders, unaffected by his visual threat. She was tired of playing along. Korbin didn't blame her, but at the same time, he needed her to behave.

He sighed. That was something he had no control over.

"What?" she asked. "It happens all the time. You'll never understand. You will *never* get how totally inadequate I feel when you guys do this. I mean," she pointed to the general's side, "it's not just you guys. It's all men, but come on!" She pointed to herself. "I'm right *here*."

You've probably got a bigger dick than any of these guys. Pandora snickered. *Except for the black guy. We all know he's packin'.*

Katie didn't reply. Their agreement had lasted one minute and thirty-seven seconds.

New world record.

I mean, if you really *want to find out I can muster one up and you can try it on for size*, Pandora said. *It might take a little bit to get used to, but hell...you could slap the shit out of a demon with it.*

Katie wanted to yell at her, but she knew now wasn't the time or place. She just continued to ignore her instead, waiting for the party to start.

Korbin shook his head, rubbed his face, and groaned. Katie looked at the general, who had maintained a straight face for a moment but now finally let go and started to laugh.

The other guys followed suit, but the colonel just sat there staring at Katie in annoyance.

When Brushwood finally settled down, he pulled a handkerchief from his pocket and wiped the sweat from his forehead. "Okay, point taken, Miss Maddison. These two gentlemen are here from military support and infrastructure. They are civilian contractors who work solely for the government and have passed rigorous security checks. Charles Butler comes to us from a major ammunition manufacturer, and Travis Novack is from the advanced metallurgical arena. They have both been thoroughly briefed on not only the demon incursions, the latest intel, and what we do versus what you do, but also they have been given the basic information on what your company does. They are here to help; to help *you* specifically, which in turn will help *us* as well as the other mercenary teams. Obviously, weapons are very important right now, and if we need to assist you to keep a steady flow coming then that is what we will do. Since the military is technically not allowed to help mercenaries in this manner, we looked to our civilian contractors."

Katie just stared at them, unsure what to say. She had just brought this need up to Korbin, and now the answer was being handed to them—but from someone that she really didn't trust, no matter what deals they had made.

She kept her guard up for her group, as Korbin did for the rest of the mercenaries.

"Mr. Butler, our ammunition man, is available to bring you whatever the hell you need in order for you to more efficiently and effectively produce those bullets," General Brushwood continued. "We have special machines at our disposal that allow us to rapidly produce rounds. We are of course offering to bring these to you at no charge. Mr. Novack is the world's preeminent specialist on new and unique metals. I just want to make it clear to you that in no way, shape, or form am I trying to steal what you guys are doing. I know that these gentlemen will be working at your site, but you need to think of the possibility of something happening to Joshua. What if he dies? I don't want the world to be fucked because we didn't do everything possible to ensure that this process continued. Since he is the *only* person in the world—that we know of—who has this knowledge, we need to protect him, but also back up that knowledge for the future."

Katie poured a glass of water and took a sip as she glanced at Korbin. Though it was her company, this had to do with her and Korbin. She was going to let him make the first response. He cleared his throat and sat forward, his hands pressed together on the table in front of him.

"Unfortunately, after what we found out today in the meeting I have to agree with General Brushwood," Korbin began. "We cannot let the one thing that may save us in this war, be lost forever because we were too unwilling to trust to back up the information."

"If I may," Mr. Butler interjected. "We have at our fingertips highly advanced machines to produce rounds. Not only do they output at the fastest pace in the business, but they are capable of working with materials most other machines cannot—and that includes, I'm sure, some we haven't even tried yet. What I am offering is to provide my expertise to customize these machines right on the floor of your factory. I can come there, figure out the specs, and make them work efficiently with whatever special metal you have in mind."

"Right." Katie peered at him. "But once we have these machines, what's stopping you from rebuilding the process back here at this base?"

Butler opened his mouth, then closed it. His brows pulled together and he looked at her strangely. The general cleared his throat and looked the other way, taking a sip of water. No one else said a word; they just let her contemplate the question she had just asked. After a few moments, she rolled her eyes at her own stupidity.

"Okay," she exclaimed, shaking her head. "I'm the dumbass here. Obviously, you already have the machines on your floor for your own business. You aren't building anything from scratch for me. I get it—you just want to help."

Butler shook his head and smirked and Katie put up a hand and stared at the others.

"I'm having to relearn a little bit here myself," she told them in embarrassment. "Please give me time, okay?"

Everyone but the colonel smiled at Katie, realizing that this time *she* was the problem. Korbin slapped her on the back a couple of times and she shook her head, trying to get her footing.

Apparently she wasn't thinking before she spoke today —well, she usually didn't, but she tried in mixed company.

She took another sip of her water and looked at the metallurgist.

"So how about you?" Katie asked. "What is your role in all this?"

"Well." He coughed. "Sorry. I'll be able to help with any issues you might have with the equipment and the special metal. But also I'm in charge of creating and building new R&D labs that need to use new metals—strong metals. The company I work for is loaning me to you to see if I can help figure out how the metal can be used in ways other than just for weapons. I've heard that it's incredibly strong, can hold a sharp edge, and has some destructive qualities when it comes to the demons' bodies."

He has had some kind of anatomical opportunities to try out a few special knives, Pandora grumped.

"You could say that," Katie told Novack, ignoring Pandora. "But if we choose to do this, all of that can be explained to you back at our facilities."

"Of course," Novack agreed. "We are here to help; I want to make that clear. From what we were told in the brief, it seems that this alliance between the two organizations could prove to be—not only beneficial but a savior for the rest of us. We weren't aware something so dire was happening, and we want to help in any way we can."

"'Dire' is not even close," Katie replied, staring into Novack's eyes. "And we really hope this doesn't fail." She glanced at Korbin. "For both groups' sake."

Damian approached the bed, flicking holy water over the girl's body. Every time the water hit her it sizzled and smoked, and she wailed loudly. The girl sat straight up in the bed and rotated her head slowly toward Damian.

"*Sacerdos get de!*"

"No," Damian yelled, "I will *not* leave. Tell me what you want with this girl! How did you get inside her?"

"*Et stulti ea paulo puero ludos. Et aviam ei si vocare posse rati sunt, sed eheu obtinuit me,*" the demon hissed.

"They summoned you? How?" Damian demanded.

"*A ludum, ludum speculum aliquis stultus. Vocaverunt eos et daemonis nesciunt. Modicum et iam non ego scio quod non reliquit, ut domum palatum parum onto eam moratum atque meam.*"

Damian gritted his teeth, angered by the way the demon talked about this girl. He didn't understand what "game" the demon was talking about. The only one *he* had ever heard of to talk to the spirits was a Ouija board, and he had long ago concluded that it was nothing more than a toy company's hoax.

He knew how dangerous mirrors could be in the working of magic, but had never heard of a child's toy with those capabilities.

"A game?" Damian whispered, turning to stare at Eric.

"What? I don't speak Latin. I don't know what they are saying."

"A game?" Damian repeated louder. "The demon said he was summoned through some sort of children's *mirror* game."

"Oh…*shit.*" Eric shook his head. "There is a new game out. It's a mirror with letters on it, and they say you can talk to spirits through it. I saw the commercial for it during the afternoon cartoons."

The ghost hunters looked at him with questioning expressions.

Eric stared at them, realizing he just admitted he watched afternoon cartoons as a grown-assed man. He was glad he hadn't mentioned the soaps he was obsessed with. They would have been *really* surprised by that.

"Hey, don't judge me," he admonished, wagging his finger at them. "My man card is in my pocket and it plans to stay there. Besides, I am not the one running around in silly uniforms looking for spirits in people's attics, okay?"

The three looked at each other and shrugged, figuring that maybe he had a point.

They wore matching tracksuits with the company logo on the front and carried around strange equipment all the time. Still, he watched cartoons, which was something that couldn't be ignored.

Damian shook his head and rolled his eyes, turning back to the girl who continued to growl and writhe in the bed. He opened his bible, took a deep breath, and began the exorcism.

"*Anima Christi sanctificare me voluistis: Corpus Christi, nisi mihi; Sanguis Christi eius inebrient me; Aquam de latere Christi lava me Dicendum quod passio Christi, confirma me; O bone Jesu, exaudi me; inebriate protege me separari a te ab uno malo, libera me: in hora mortis meae voca me: et iube me venire ad te, ut cum Sanctis tuis laudem te in saecula saeculorum.* Amen."

The girl screamed in agony, but the demon clutched her soul tightly. Damian grimaced and flipped another page of his book and, stepping forward, he placed his hand on her forehead. She wriggled, her arms out to her sides, her eyes rolled back until just the whites showed.

"*Dominus meus, vos autem potentes omnia, tu es Deus, tu pater. Nos obsecro, et, intercedente pro nobis auxilium de ordine Archangelorum Michael, Gabriel et Raphael, ad liberandos etiam fratrum nostrórum, qui in malo et servus est. Sanctis caeli succurrat,*" Damian yelled, marking a cross across her forehead.

She screamed again, but this time her chest arched and light came from her open mouth. She shook violently and Damian released her head, set his book on the nightstand, and sprinkled holy water over her, then pulled up his sleeves and held his cross out in front of him.

His presence became more intense as he shouted, "*Daemonium dimittere eam! Dimittere eam. Vade ad vidisse igneos puteos horrendam ex inferno, et maneat ibi in aeternum ardenti in peccatum.*"

The girl's head snapped to the right and she looked at Damian with red eyes. Holding the cross tightly, he roared the words over and over again. She screamed so loudly the glass in the mirror across from her bed shattered and hundreds of shards fell to the floor.

Suddenly there was a wind in the room, but Damian held his cross tightly.

"Fuck you," the demon screamed in a deep, angry voice. "I will see you in *hell!*"

The girl's eyes flashed red and she fell back onto the bed, her body returning to its normal posture and color.

Damian breathed deeply and slowly lowered the cross,

then put it back inside his jacket. He glanced at the ghost hunters, who were gaping at him in shock. Eric had the same look on his face when he looked in that direction.

"Was our date romantic enough?" Damian joked, then walked out.

5

The general decided that now would be a good time to break for lunch and announced, "We have catered sandwiches and fruit. Help yourselves." He then pulled a cigar out of his pocket and chewed on the end, knowing he couldn't smoke it inside the facility. Colonel Jehovivich turned to the general, then glanced across the room at Katie and the others.

"General, may I speak with you for a moment?" She flicked her eyes to the corner. "Over there, in private?"

"I suppose." He pushed the chair back and walked to the corner. "What's this about, Colonel?"

"I don't know how you could find this *okay*," she began, looking at Katie and back at Brushwood. "She made a damned demon claw out of her *nail*. Don't you think that is a bit too much? Who's the enemy here? We have killed infected for less than that in the field. Now we are allowing a merc to march into our facilities and put on a show like it's some badge of honor, showing off what the demon inside of her can do?"

"Calm down." The general sighed.

Her voice hissed. "Calm *down*? How can I *calm down* when I am watching you negotiate with a woman who is obviously hiding something from us although she's supposed to be an ally? How in the world is she going to ally with *us* when she and her demon are so close? How can we trust her to do the right thing when she is clearly consorting with her demon? And she's changed. Her body is…different from the last time I saw her, and the last time I checked that was a definite reason for concern when working with the Damned."

The general rolled his unlit cigar around with his fingers and watched Katie as she talked and joked with Korbin and Calvin.

He was aware she could be dangerous, and he knew that the way she handled her demon was not at all typical of how most of the Damned did, but at the same time, none of *them* had been able to do what she had done.

She was a beast in the field—a killing machine—and she never wavered, not once that he had seen. He had pledged alliance, and though he had kept things at arm's length he needed to give credit where credit was due, otherwise they would never get anywhere. He looked at the colonel for a moment, noting the anger on her face and the fear in her eyes.

"Let me ask you a question." He took the cigar from his mouth. "Do we need to understand how to kill humans?"

The colonel opened her mouth, then shut it and shook her head, looking at him in confusion. "Well, no. I think we understand *exactly* how to kill humans. In fact, we have known that since we were created."

"That's right." He nodded. "I don't think Katie needs to tell us how to kill humans either. And if she was our enemy, why would she be trying to help us kill her and her team?"

"I... Well... She..." The colonel stumbled over her words, frustrated by the general's seeming indifference to her *very fucking valid* concerns.

"She wouldn't, and she isn't," the general finished. "Colonel, you and I are going to have a discussion when this meeting is over."

The general walked back to his seat, sat down, and handed his plate to one of the airmen helping to clean up lunch. Colonel Jehovivich just stood there for a moment, completely shocked by the general's response.

She had worked with him for years; even transferred to that unit with him to remain his right-hand person...and this was the first time he had ever reprimanded her. She closed her mouth and gritted her teeth, then walked back to the table and sat down. She glared at Katie, who looked at her and smiled widely when she noticed her irritation.

"All right," the general interjected, rubbing his hands together. "Everyone ready to continue?"

Everyone nodded, so the general flipped his folder open and read the notes he had taken. Jehovivich just sat there, determined not to say a word for the rest of the meeting.

The general had made his position very clear, and she wasn't going to get herself into hotter water if she could avoid it.

"So not only will these two men put in machines, they

will help you build a rapid manufacturing facility at your base," the general explained. "Everything you will need to enable Joshua to mass-produce metals and bullets, which will free up some of his time to work on other weapons of your choosing."

They sat there for several hours discussing the ins and outs of the new facility.

It was important that they nail down all the details before they were done so that they could continue on without further meetings.

Everyone in that room was very busy with their respective duties, and the manufacturing of those bullets was one of the top things to be put in place—especially if the demons were training and planning at the same pace.

"Hey," Katie whispered, turning to Korbin. "How good is your relationship with Stephanie?"

Calvin snickered, covering his mouth. She locked eyes with him for a few seconds, then looked away, ignoring his childish behavior.

Korbin lifted an eyebrow, unsure why she was asking.

"I want to know because we are going to be dumping a lot of stuff on her land," Katie explained. "I would prefer that we are clear it stays with the base. We can't allow friendships or relationships to get in the way. You know how important it is that all of this stays a secret, and not just now. It needs to stay secret for as long as it takes to defeat these bastards, even if you and I aren't around to see that."

"I see." Korbin thought for a moment.

Katie put her finger to her chin. "We could always build somewhere else, like buy a piece of property and have it secured like the base but not attached. I mean, it will be a little more difficult to protect since we aren't there twenty-four hours a day, but it would keep us from having to bring it up with her, and the facility would be brand new."

Korbin shook his head. "No. We don't even have the manpower to run our base properly when we are fully staffed. We can't afford to send protection to *another* place. I'll negotiate with Stephanie for the land to belong to Korbin's Killers, LLC. That way we'll own all of it and it will stay safe no matter what."

When the exorcism was over, Damian and Eric headed out to the SUV and climbed inside. Damian put his bible back into the bag and set it in the backseat and glanced at Eric, who looked like he'd never seen a crazy demon before.

Damian chuckled and patted him on the shoulder. "It's all right. It's all over."

"I think I will have nightmares about that girl for the rest of my life." Eric shuddered.

"Ha. No, you won't." Damian snickered. "You should see it when Katie is there. It's *really* terrifying then."

Eric shook his head. "I don't even want to think about it."

Damian pulled out his phone. "I gotta call Stephanie about the game."

"This is Stephanie," she answered after two rings.

"Hey, it's Damian."

Her voice was casually chipper. "Hey there, how did it go? Pull some creepy demon from a person's body? Did he turn his head in a circle and projectile-vomit?" Then she whispered so loudly Eric could hear, "Did Eric get coated in it?"

"They don't really do that." Damian laughed. "Although they get pretty close sometimes. But yeah, we got that all taken care of and no about Eric. The problem is, we figured out there is a board game out there called Mirror Mirror that may be where that demon came from. It's a kid's game she played on Saturday with her friends, and she came home with the nasty demon I just sent back to hell while he yelled profanities at me."

"Oh, that sounds wonderful." Stephanie snickered.

"I need you to get ahold of Korbin and ask him what to do, especially since he is with the general," Damian said. "Or at least that's where I think he is."

"I can do that," Stephanie agreed. "This could turn into a huge problem."

"Hopefully they haven't left yet, so Korbin and the general can speak face to face. We'll be back soon."

Damian hung up and shook his head, glancing up as the ghost hunters carried their video equipment to the van. Two of them looked as shocked as Eric, but the leader didn't seem to be fazed at all.

"I gotta go talk to them really fast," Damian told Eric. "Just stay here and relax for a minute."

"I will *not* argue with you," Eric replied, shaking his head.

Damian got out of the SUV and walked over to the three, watching them put the last of their equipment in the van. When the leader turned around he shook Damian's hand, excited about the footage they had gotten.

"Thanks for everything," he said.

"No problem," Damian replied. "I just need you guys to remember to make sure that neither my face nor Eric's is on *any* of those videos you release, or you and I will have another discussion—and I'll bring Katie with me."

"Right," they all said, terrified.

Eric chuckled; his window was down, so he heard them talking. Damian went back to the SUV and climbed into the driver's seat, then started the car and headed out of the neighborhood.

He realized Eric was staring at him with his eyebrows raised.

"What?" Damian asked.

"Why would you threaten them with Katie?"

"Because you aren't as impressive as she is when it comes to scaring people," Damian replied. "Trust me, they've seen what she can do, and they do *not* want to mess with what they saw."

"I don't doubt you in the least," Eric agreed.

Stephanie sat there for a moment trying to figure out the best way to contact Korbin, since he was probably still in his meeting.

She sent him a text first, telling him it was vital he call her before he left the general. She sat there for fifteen minutes waiting for a call, a text, *anything* to show he had seen that, but he didn't respond at all.

Finally she picked up the phone and dialed his number.

"Yes," he answered abruptly. "I am in the middle of a very important meeting right now."

"Damian and Eric went out on a possession call a bit ago," Stephanie explained, momentarily ignoring his piss-poor attitude. "When they had finished—successfully—they called and told me about a new game on the market called Mirror Mirror. It allows you to contact spirits, and that game was how the demon got into this kid's body. It is sold all over the world, or so it said when I looked it up."

Korbin, voice still terse, asked. "How does he know it was the game?"

"The demon told him before he shoved him back to hell," Stephanie replied dryly. "The kids thought they were going to contact the girl's grandmother, but that wasn't what happened at all."

"Jesus," Korbin replied, sighing over the phone. "What a fucking mess. All right, thanks for letting me know, I'll approach the general about it."

"Oh, and Korbin?" Stephanie said quickly before he hung up.

"Yeah?" he asked, obviously ready to end the call.

"You would think that by now, between work and the personal thing you would trust my judgment enough to not question me or be nasty when I think there is a good enough reason to interrupt you," she told him. "Next time *remember* that."

She hung up.

Korbin pulled the phone from his ear and looked at the screen, surprised by Stephanie's reaction.

He hadn't *meant* to disrespect her, but now that he thought about it he could see exactly why she might be upset with him. He went back to the table and sat down, waiting for a good moment to interject. When the general finished with the topic he was on, Korbin spoke.

"That was a call from the team that went out on a demon exorcism," Korbin announced. "Apparently there is a new game out there called Mirror Mirror, and it's allowing demons to jump into bodies. My priest just exorcised a high-school-aged girl."

The general growled, mangling his cigar, and slammed his fist on the table. "Goddamn it! So, *what?* We now have to worry about a fucking game that has gone national?"

"Actually it's gone international, from what I've been told," Korbin replied.

The general turned to Colonel Jehovivich. "I want you on a bird, and by that I mean an airplane...or hell, a fucking *bird*—whatever will get you to this company right now to shut it the fuck down. Then I want to understand what it's gonna take to pull that game out of circulation immediately."

"Yes, sir," she replied, standing up.

The general watched as she quickly gathered her things and raced from the room. When the door shut behind her he leaned forward, rubbing his face. His unlit and barely-intact cigar was now in his hand.

"I cannot *believe* the kind of bullshit luck we have been having on a daily basis," he told them. Every time he turned around there was something insane happening.

He looked at Korbin, who was shaking his head in irritation. "With all the fucking problems we have, you're telling me now that somehow our fellow idiots...I mean, Americans, have introduced a way to pull demons through a *game*?" The general groaned and leaned his head against the back of his chair.

He looked at the men in suits. "I think this meeting is over. You two, schedule your arrival with Katie before you leave. I've got to get to my office and attempt to pull children's games off the shelves before we have a rash of insane twelve-year-olds running around."

Everyone shook the general's hand and he stomped out of the room. Katie looked at Korbin and Calvin, who shrugged.

"We should be at your base by Thursday afternoon," Butler told them.

"Sounds good." Katie nodded. "It's time to make some weapons, 'cause I got a list a mile long of demons waiting for one between the eyes."

6

Katie, Korbin, and Calvin walked out of the building and stopped outside for a minute before heading toward the chopper. Korbin looked grumpy as hell and was staring into space. Katie tilted her head and stepped in front of him, then waved her hand in front of his face.

"You in there, chief?" she asked.

Korbin's eyes focused on her and he sighed. "Yeah, I'm here."

"What's wrong with you?"

"Stephanie snapped at me for being short with her on the phone," Korbin grumped. "She called in the middle of a meeting, so it was a natural reaction. She acted like a jilted girlfriend, which was exactly what I was trying to avoid. That was why I didn't want to ask her out. I didn't want there to be any weirdness in the kitchen."

"Stephanie reacted perfectly naturally," Katie replied. "She didn't react like a girlfriend, she reacted like a human who just got her ass jumped because she was doing her job. I would be sad for her if she hadn't said something smart back to you. Hell, *I* would have fucking let you have it with both barrels."

Katie blew a wisp of hair out of her face. "You have to remember that she took care of her own business—and straightened *ours* out—well before we ever asked her to. You aren't thinking *before* you react. Sometimes you forget that we are under stress too, Korbin, and that when you snap at us we want to kick you in the teeth."

"You're right." Korbin sighed and glanced around. "I've been out of my element lately; I'll be the first to admit it. Working with the government has thrown me off. I have been here a long time, at least for a demon hunter, so I know what the government has done to us. Acting like it never happened and moving forward with this alliance is difficult for me. I'm waiting for the other shoe to drop."

"You cannot continue to think that way," Katie told him. "I understand it's important to be cautious. I get that—and I *am* being cautious—but it's not a good thing when you are constantly looking for something wrong and taking it out on your own people. You need to take a deep breath and believe that right now this is the best option we have. We need to stick together as a team here, Korbin, so that if the worst happens we still have each other. Otherwise we are all as good as dead. Most of the time it's not the skill that wins battles, it's teamwork—and ours is top-notch because we are friends."

"I know," Korbin agreed. "And now I need to figure out how to apologize to Stephanie—and actually get her to accept it."

"Don't make excuses," Calvin supplied. "That's one of the biggest things; you don't want to make excuses for your behavior. No matter why you did it, you want her to know you feel bad for snapping at her.. Otherwise it's just going to get worse."

Katie turned to him, surprise evident on her face. "Look at you, knowing about women." She laughed.

"I know a thing or two from my past life," he told her, straightening his shirt. "I can be a real gentleman when I want to be."

Speaking of gentlemen. Pandora preened. *There were at least six very hot men commenting on the bodacious body that walked past them a minute ago.*

I need to come here more often, Katie replied. *I mean, seriously...a girl could grow a huge head here.*

Or give it. Pandora giggled. *I do know that we just made a deal with the human equivalent of the devil and we got checked out by at least ten men while we were here, which means a celebration is in order.*

"I suggest *donuts*," Katie exclaimed excitedly...and aloud.

Korbin and Calvin stopped talking and looked at Katie in confusion. She was smiling to herself, kicking rocks and not paying them any attention.

"You think I should get *donuts* for Stephanie?" Korbin asked. "I didn't think she was a huge fan, but if you think she is I'm not gonna argue."

Katie looked at the guys. Once she realized that she had said that out loud there was no going back. She was hell-bent on getting delicious donuts, something Pandora hadn't asked for in at least a week.

"Well, sure." Katie smiled. "Every girl loves sugar. You

can give them to Stephanie too, but I'm suggesting *I* need donuts right now."

"What, are we gonna land the chopper on the roof of a donut shop?" Calvin asked. "You want us to climb down ladders, maybe?"

"No." Katie giggled. "Hold on one second."

She walked over to a group of airmen who were watching from a distance. It looked like she was flirting with them, but Korbin and Calvin couldn't hear what she said. Finally one of them came over and handed her something small.

She kissed him on the cheek before walking back toward Calvin and Korbin. When she reached them, she revealed the set of keys in her hand. They went to the parking lot and beeped the alarm until finally they found his SUV in the back corner.

"So?" Katie asked, climbing into the back seat.

"Absolutely," Calvin agreed, putting the car in drive.

"You can always count me in for donuts," Korbin assured them.

Calvin headed into the small town that bordered the base and finally found a locally-owned donut shop.

Katie was like a kid in a candy shop, and Korbin was determined to take a ton of donuts back to the base. He now had it in his head that he would win Stephanie back with the cream-filled chocolate glazed. They ended up leaving the place with five dozen donuts.

These better not be those damned potato-flour ones, Pandora grumped. *They don't heat up well. They just get mushy. It's so gross.*

"Excuse me." Katie addressed the girl behind the counter. "Do these donuts warm up well?"

"They sure do." She smiled. "I heat mine almost every morning."

She gets to eat donuts every morning? Pandora scoffed. *That lucky fucking bitch! Why couldn't I have entered her body? I could be in donut heaven every day and never have to worry about fighting other demons with bitchy attitudes.*

Forget the donut every morning and your comment about my attitude, and think about how tomorrow morning you will be able to warm the donut up and savor every delicious bite. That is if they don't all get eaten tonight, Katie replied. *They promised that these donuts are good for heating up, and I doubt they'd lie to me. They see the truth I am seeking, and I have found it for you, so can we go now? We need to get back to base before the demon war is over.*

Yes, yes, Pandora griped. *Pushing me and shit. Besides, if they are lying I will exact revenge. I know how to hang people from hooks and torture them with hot oil. I know how to remove every piece of skin while keeping the person alive long enough to feel the pain. I am not against waterboarding, but I don't use water. I use blood.*

Whoa, whoa, crazy ass. Katie chuckled. *You need to keep a lid on your homicidal tendencies while you are in my body.*

Hey, when you lie to me, you are asking for capital punishment, Pandora growled.

You demons are hypocrites, Katie told her. *Every single one of you goes out and lies, lies, lies to everyone you meet, but let someone do it to you and you fly off the handle. Peeling skin off bodies and trying to kill people—I think you need to think about your attitude, young lady.*

Pandora gasped. *You are patronizing me. How dare you?*

I am not patronizing you. Katie laughed. *I'm just letting you know that you are bat-shit crazy.*

I can show you crazy, Pandora assured her. *I can make you see tiny pink elephants and create some disease where you strip naked anytime you are in public. I can see you now, running around with your titties bouncing up and down, screaming about the pink elephants chasing you. It would be fucking hilarious.*

And you would be right there inside me, Katie ground out. *We could ride off to the crazy house together where they don't have donuts...or anything else edible either. It's also pretty noisy, and they make you wear a uniform.*

Dammit, Pandora growled. *Your logic has thwarted me again. I will get you one of these days.*

She started to cackle like a mad scientist and Katie had to turn away from the others and hold back her laugh.

At least Pandora had a sense of humor.

The general watched from the next room as Katie, Calvin, and Korbin borrowed a car and headed toward the town. He couldn't quite figure out what they would want in town, but then again he really didn't care. He'd stayed behind to have a couple of words with the two contractors. He knew they weren't going to be as helpful as they had seemed in the meeting.

"Guys!" the general called, stepping into the lobby.

"General," the two men returned, nodding.

"May I have a word with you for just a moment?"

"Sure," they responded and followed him back into the room.

General Brushwood closed the doors behind him and looked both of them up and down. The smile faded from his face and he pulled a fresh cigar out of his pocket and stuck the end in his mouth. The guys looked at each other, then back at the general.

"I want to make something clear to you gentlemen," he told them. "I am not in any way trying to get you to learn everything Katie's people can do so you can steal it."

"We know…"

"If that lady…" the general interrupted and pointed to the west. "If she so much as *believes* that you are trying to steal her stuff? I can promise you that you will be *very* sorry. Imagine what would happen if she grew a nail six inches long and stuck it up your ass?"

They looked at the general with wide eyes and then at each other, swallowing hard.

"So," the general continued, "if your bosses suggest you need to do some spying, tell them to stop that shit right there. If you find that they don't want to stop, get *me* involved. If you don't and your lives are snuffed out in some horrible fashion, expect nothing more than an unmarked grave out in the desert. And guess what?" He smiled, but it didn't reach his eyes. "You will already *be* out in the desert, so they won't have to go very far to dump your bodies."

"Everything is coming together perfectly," T'Chezz

announced as he paced around Moloch's office. "I didn't realize it was possible to fight fire with fire. They went in there and showed those Damned assholes who was boss. They may not have killed all of them like I wanted them to, but they sent the message that I will not back down. I will not run because they have some silly little weapons that hurt. We are fucking *demons*, for Lucifer's sake. We will show them who is stronger and smarter, and we are not afraid to die."

Moloch watched as T'Chezz wandered back and forth, his thoughts reeling with exquisite battle scenes.

Never mind that he was giving no credit to Moloch and his people; the ones who actually did the killing.

Instead, T'Chezz was getting a larger and larger ego, and had now shifted his attention to how to make his effort more expansive.

"We could train so many like this," T'Chezz continued, his arms wide. "We could build an army, and they would wipe out these bastards so fast the humans wouldn't even know what had hit them. I will be the master of that world. I will rain blood on their fragile little bodies, laughing all the way. I will take Earth over, and Lucifer will be more than happy to give me a seat at the level that I *belong* on."

Moloch lifted his naked and scaly black brow and let out a deep sigh, but he decided to just let him get it out of his system.

Moloch could have squashed T'Chezz in a heartbeat, but at that moment the lesser demon was the perfect one to get him closer to winning on Earth. T'Chezz had already put in a lot of work, and he wasn't going to stop there.

Moloch just had to keep T'Chezz from doing something stupid.

"We should invade Chicago," T'Chezz blurted, nodding to himself.

Like that.

"You are quite the ambitious one," Moloch exclaimed. "That is a quality all leaders have. You remind me of a younger version of myself. But I think that until we get a stronger army, we should stick to *smaller* towns—maybe a thousand humans to begin with. Something that is not close to any of the merc bases. Something off by itself."

"Yesss… You are right." T'Chezz nodded. "Make sure that I am ready; it is better that way. Thank you, Moloch, for your guidance."

T'Chezz wasn't even looking in Moloch's direction.

"Of course." Moloch sneered. "For the next operation you will want to take a handful of Level Fives, or maybe a Level-Four powerhouse even, along with you."

"I really like that idea," T'Chezz agreed as he paced, glancing to Moloch a couple of times. "I did find directing the troops from my home base *very* effective; more effective than anything I have done so far. Maybe I should stay there; move them like pawns in a chess game."

Moloch shook his head and rolled his eyes when T'Chezz turned his back to him. Controlling troops from the base was a cop-out.

"You mean keep yourself safe, you giant pussy," Moloch muttered under his breath.

7

K atie stepped into the doorway of Joshua's building and smiled as she leaned against the doorframe.

Lights brightened the place up. Joshua had classical music playing and he hummed along, not even noticing that she was there.

He had made himself a nice little home, or at least as homey as people like them could make a place. She wandered in and looked at the framed pictures on the table while she waited for his attention to shift from the sword he was constructing.

"Oh." Joshua raised his goggles and smiled at Katie. "I'm sorry, I didn't hear you come in."

"It's fine." She smiled back, nodding toward the sword. "I didn't want to disturb you while you were working."

"Not a problem." He turned off the machine and set the sword on the table. "I was ready for a break anyway, *AND*," he wiggled his eyebrows, "I have something for you."

"Really?" Katie was excited, but she hadn't wanted to ask since she knew how hard Joshua was worked.

"Yep." Joshua grinned as he pressed the security lift button and waited for their armory cabinet to appear.

Once it had locked in place he put in the code that opened the door and pulled out her new quarterstaff, which was even more intricately designed than she had thought it would be.

She walked forward as he beamed at her with excitement in his eyes.

"So, I gave it everything you wanted," he told her, turning a nob at the end and pressing a button. "It's got the metal at both ends for added protection, and I did a few more modifications."

He grabbed the center and pulled it apart, holding up two batons. He held them by the ends and pressed buttons, waving them as knives popped out. Katie clapped her hands and jumped up and down in excitement.

"I figured, why have just one badass weapon when you can have two?" He grinned.

This. Is. Amazing, Pandora cooed. *I'm seriously getting wet just looking at this weapon.*

"Wow, Joshua!" Katie took the batons from him and clicked the buttons that pulled in the knives. "This is *amazing.*"

"I carved your name into the side of each," he pointed out.

Katie turned the baton over and looked at the intricate design carefully etched into the wood.

She smiled, running her hand over it, and decided that this was the best thing she had ever been given.

Crazy how her wants and needs had changed. Just a couple of years before she would have loved a new volleyball or a better pair of Nikes. Now, well *now* it was a badass demon-killing quarterstaff that got her energy pumping.

Katie locked the two pieces back together and stepped into an open space. She warmed up with her staff, swinging it through a couple of katas to get used to its weight and balance.

Katie clicked the buttons and the longer blades emerged as she continued her form.

She stabbed, then rotated in place and attacked with the other blade. She twisted the staff and the two pieces came apart, allowing her to attack in two directions.

Slamming them together, she twisted again. However, she didn't succeed in locking them and stumbled. "Gotta work on that," she murmured and slowed down, her smile lighting her eyes.

Pandora laughed. *I'd love to shove these up T'Chezz's ass.*

Hell, yeah, Katie replied. *Then maybe you would be free to go back home and not have to worry about his ass.*

Yeah, Pandora replied quietly and with a forced chuckle.

Katie noticed that Pandora had gone silent, but she took the time to thank Joshua before putting her new weapon through her belt. She made a mental note to do some design work to find something to hold it down better; maybe something strapped to her thigh. She headed back outside and looked out over the desert, leaving Joshua to his work.

It was a beautiful day. The wind had even died down.

I wish every day was this gorgeous. I could kick ass extra hard with the sun shining on me, Katie told Pandora.

Mmhmm, Pandora replied.

Okay, what's up? You got really quiet.

Nothing, she said in a fake upbeat tone. *I just want to think for a bit. Nothing serious.*

All right. Katie was curious, but not enough to push. *That will last as long as it takes to reach the kitchen and warm up more donuts.*

Katie went down into the tunnels and dropped her staff off in the practice room, then headed to the kitchen. She hadn't noticed Pandora's tone.

She pulled a box of donuts from the fridge and stuck three of them in the microwave, whistling while she waited, then inhaled the scent wafting from the plate.

"Smells like my kind of lunch," Katie exclaimed.

I know, right? Pandora chuckled. *Gotta get the donuts in for the day.*

Pandora's tone was playful but serious. She wasn't in the mood to play around, and she didn't want Katie asking questions.

So she forced a snarky comment and tried to enjoy the donuts.

Katie licked her fingers, thinking about the coming days and wondering what was in store for her and Pandora. It was rare that she had quiet time. She was used to Pandora's constant chatter, especially during donut time, so she was happy to have this bit of peace.

She never knew when the next call would come. When the next demon would break through to take out more of her comrades or innocents, those living their lives with no clue of what was really going on behind the scenes.

She still couldn't believe she had been one of those

people for most of her life—until Pandora changed everything. She liked her new life though, and had made peace with her future.

Katie wasn't sure what she would do if things changed; if Pandora was gone and she went back to a life like the one she'd had before.

It would be a lot less exciting...not that she'd remember this one, that was for damn sure.

Katie pushed back from the table and rubbed her belly. That had been a hell of a lot of donuts—since she had gone back for another serving.

She couldn't help but notice that Pandora hadn't helped out with the metabolizing this time. She was about to comment on it when the intercom buzzed. She cringed at the loud sound and sighed.

"Attention: there has been a new incursion," Stephanie called over the intercom. "Please report to the call room for more information."

Katie put her hands on the table and pushed herself to her feet. *Well, good thing I feel like a donut zombie right now.*

Huh? Oh crap, sorry! Pandora kicked Katie's metabolism into overdrive.

Thanks, friend, Katie said as she skipped out of the room and down the hall. *Sugar high metabolizing. I think I'll be at level eleven for a while.*

She rounded the corner and slowed down to enter the call room. Stephanie was behind the desk writing something down and looked at Katie with exhaustion on her face. Katie raised her eyebrows and sat down in front of her.

"I guess I'm the first one," Katie said.

"Yeah. I don't even know if the intercom works in all of the rooms."

"So, what is this new call all about?"

"It's on a small wooded ranch two hours east-northeast of Las Vegas," Stephanie read from the paper. "It doesn't really give any detailed information about what to expect, but HQ sent out the call."

Pandora sniffed around for a moment before speaking up.

You need to take this, Pandora told her with a serious tone. *Bring your new weapon and specifically ask for Damian to go.*

Why Damian? Katie asked.

Just trust me...go get the priest, she responded.

All right, Katie said to Pandora and looked at Stephanie. "I'll take it, and I'll grab Damian too."

"Sounds good," Stephanie agreed, staring at the computer. "Put in your earbuds, I'll send info as I get it. I'm gonna grab something to eat, though. I'm starving."

Katie nodded and headed out of the room. There was something about Pandora's tone that made her uneasy, but the call had to be taken. She went down the tunnels to the sanctuary, where she found Damian finishing a prayer. He stood and straightened his jacket, looking at Katie with a raised eyebrow.

"What's up?"

"There's a call," Katie told him. "It's about two hours from here on a ranch."

"Damn intercom system." Damian shook his head. "They need to just start hitting the button for the bells."

"Yeah." Katie looked at the floor. "Hey, listen, Pandora is really insistent that the two of us head out to this one. She wanted me to grab you and my new quarterstaff and fly over in the chopper."

"Why?"

"I don't know, but I trust her enough."

Gee, thanks, Pandora grumbled.

"I'd be fine with that, but I don't know how to fly the helicopter. Korbin is gonna have to go with us. As of this morning, we don't have the pilot anymore," Damian replied.

Shit, Pandora hissed. *Korbin...the guy who has reservations about you. Great. I guess it was bound to happen one day. Listen, you need to have a heart-to-heart with Korbin while you're in the air about totally and completely trusting you.*

I don't know, Katie said doubtfully. *That's a big ask.*

Fine, but if you don't think Korbin is willing to keep your secret, I'll just show you something new some other time, Pandora told her. *I can't do it in front of Korbin if I can't trust him.*

I think he might feel the same way about us, Katie remarked with a sigh, looking up at the neon cross. *Strange things are afoot, and he is just being cautious.*

Caution is good, but trust is better, Pandora replied.

The day had been a long one for Calvin, with endless tasks he had to complete.

When he was done he headed over to the training area thinking he was just going to clean weapons, but he ended up doing a bit more.

Things were weighing heavily on everyone's minds. There had been the deaths, especially Derek's, the rogue demon soldiers, and the fact that everything had steadily been increasing in difficulty and danger for quite a while. Calvin was just as tired as everyone else; not just physically, but mentally as well.

As second-in-command, he had to not only keep his spirits up but his team's spirits as well. They relied on him for a more hands-on approach then Korbin gave. That was always the way it went with the number two.

Calvin had always had the answers—and if he didn't he would find them—but recently he had been falling short in that duty.

He found himself perplexed by the information he had been given, and he looked to the others to help him figure it out.

It was new, and not just to him. These were new developments in the history of demons, which was a big thing considering it had been generations and generations since they had started to wreak havoc on Earth.

Calvin ambled through the halls, taking his time to get to the main living quarters. He had done some hardcore training earlier and was a little tired.

He reached the doorway and stopped, tilting his head to the side in confusion. Stephanie sat at the table surrounded by three boxes of donuts, and there was a lot of sugar around her mouth.

"Don't know, don't care, *don't* give me your thoughts at the moment. I'm high."

She smiled, giving zero shits about the situation she'd been caught in. Calvin looked down at the donuts and back at Stephanie with a plethora of questions in his eyes. Stephanie glared back as she grabbed another donut.

"This was Korbin's way of apologizing," she told him. She looked at a cream-filled donut. "Perhaps donuts don't last as long as roses, but they sure as hell taste better."

Calvin looked at her for a moment and she stared back straight-faced, then both of them broke into hysterical laughter. He shook his head and walked over to the table and sat down. He grabbed a donut from the box and looked at it for a moment, letting the laughter subside before taking a huge bite.

"If I were a woman this would be how I would always want a man to apologize." He chuckled.

"Then all the women in the world would be morbidly obese," Stephanie replied, raising her eyebrows. "And don't sit there and act like men don't have to apologize that much, because if they haven't been they should be."

"The donut business would definitely boom, that's for sure, and it's a hell of a lot cheaper than flowers."

"Very true." Stephanie smiled as she leaned back and patted her donut belly. "At least we would never go hungry."

Calvin thought for a moment. "We'd all have diabetes and high blood pressure, but we *wouldn't* be hungry."

Stephanie shrugged. "Meh, who cares? Our life expectancy is pretty low anyway."

"Ain't that the truth," Calvin replied, shaking his head and wiping his hands on a napkin.

They sat there quietly for several moments, not even eating. It was almost as if that lighthearted statement had landed like a ton of bricks on their shoulders. Calvin looked out the window, watching the helicopter warming up.

There was no other feeling like the one he got when he watched his team take off toward an incursion.

He always wondered who would come back.

"Can I ask you something?" Stephanie began, breaking the silence.

"Sure," he replied.

"You have known Korbin for a while, right?"

Calvin hesitated, unsure where the conversation was going to lead. He had no issues with Stephanie and Korbin being together, but he made it a rule to not get involved.

Still, he knew he was one of the few people she could talk to about their leader, so he nodded. "Yeah, quite a while. Longer than most."

"In all the time that he's been a mercenary, has he ever had a girlfriend?" she asked.

"Ha!" Calvin leaned back. "That's an easy one. Korbin has had a stick up his ass ever since he became a mercenary, I don't think his dick ever got hard unless he was killing a demon." He saw that Stephanie looked unsure about whether he was telling the truth.

He used his hands to form a circle. "No shit. A pole four inches in diameter—with splinters—rammed in there from Day One." He shook his head.

"Okayyy."

Calvin smiled and stood up to leave the room. "Give him time. He'll figure it all out. Sometimes we start out slow, but he's quick on the uptake. He'll start acting right. We are stuck in our ways here, finding what helps us survive and moving forward, not wanting to change that. He cares about you though...I can tell."

Stephanie watched as Calvin walked out of the room and out of sight. He was right; they *did* all have their own special ways of doing things. They got stuck in their habits because if they had survived that far there had to be something to it.

She reached for another donut and looked at the empty doorway.

"I'll let you off the hook *this* time, Korbin. But somehow we have to make sure you get your relationship groove back."

8

"Hell yeah!" The Enlightened was propped against the door. "We rolled in there and not one of them knew how to take it. After all the hype they met their match, and we made sure they didn't just leave and forget that."

"Fuck, yes," another agreed, his deep voice appropriate for his six-foot eight-inch body. "Did you see how I broke that one dude almost in half? He might have been the only casualty, but I'm pretty sure three or four of them will be drinking their breakfast through a straw for the near future."

The guys pulled their gear on and jacked themselves up for another ambush. They trained hard; harder than most of those in the military.

Well, at least those in the Navy and Air Force. Those folks' jobs didn't require them to lug backpacks or kick in doors.

These "Enlightened," as Moloch called them, had sparks

in their eyes for death.

They were dangerous. While they compared themselves to the Damned mercenaries, they knew they had one advantage the others didn't: they didn't care about anyone or anything. They *definitely* didn't care about the innocent, and that made them extremely dangerous.

When their gear was on they sat and talked excitedly about the next mission. They were ready to go; they just needed information on where and what their targets were. All the Enlightened had pledged their lives to Moloch, and their demons had no outside touch with the world.

They ate, slept, and breathed training, and they grew stronger every day—not just their human bodies but also their connections with their demons.

Each day was spent learning new skills until they became muscle memory, and there were no rules or artificial constraints—like morality—that kept them from using them.

"I keep picturing that one guy flying head-first into that cement wall." One of the men laughed. "It was absolutely beautiful."

"On your feet," Trenton, the leader of the Enlightened barked as he walked in.

Trenton paced in front of the men, inspecting them from head to toe. Their eyes glowed bright-red and they stared forward like soldiers.

Trenton was bigger than the rest, as well as angrier and smarter, and his demon was the highest-level among them. He had mastered his weapons, he learned faster than the others (if not by much), and Moloch looked to him to lead the troops.

"All I heard from the hallway was gloating." Trenton halted, his feet shoulder-width apart, hands behind his back. "I didn't hear *tactics*. I didn't hear silent contemplation. I heard childish giggling like you won some sort of fucking trophy."

"Sir?" Wilson, one of the Enlightened, spoke up. "To be honest, we all felt really good about how we handled the last op and how strong we have become. We are building commodities."

Trenton stared at the man like he was an idiot.

The man next to Wilson leaned over just a bit and whispered, "It's 'comradery,' dumbass!"

Wilson spoke louder. "Building *comradery*, sir!"

Trenton ran his tongue over his teeth before replying. "You don't *need* comradery," he responded, now nose to nose with the guy. "You *need* to follow orders. When you are out there you rely on yourself and the demon inside you—that is, after you rely on *me* to tell you what to do."

He looked at everyone. "That was our first fight, and yes, you did well, but you can do better. Next time will be different by leagues. They had no idea we existed during that first fight, but I can *promise* you that after the damage we did they *all* know about us now. They will not be caught with their pants down twice. They are skilled, experienced, and determined. I cannot have you underestimating their strength."

"Yes, sir," they all replied.

Trenton stepped back. "Now we have another mission, so make sure you are mentally and physically prepared. I don't have any information on where we are going; Moloch is bringing us that. Until he gets here, I will answer any questions you may have, then we can go over some tactical moves."

"We heard a rumor that there are special weapons out there. Ones that can hurt us really bad," one of the Enlightened said.

"That rumor is true," Trenton replied.

There was a burst of whispered chatter.

Trenton cut it off. "But if you think about it, *if they can hurt us the weapons will hurt these Damned as well.* You need to have faith in your skills, in your demons, and most importantly in Moloch. He will protect us; he promised that from the beginning. Sure, some of us may die in the process, but we will go down in history as heroes who fought for the freedom of everyone like us. The demons promise us a glory-filled future."

The mumbles were happy now, so Trenton let them continue.

"My demon makes me feel invincible," one of the Enlightened declared excitedly.

"Me too," another responded from the back.

"Yeah, like I could run through the flames of hell and be okay," another added.

"They do have that effect, don't they," Trenton agreed. "But you have to remember that your demon may be invincible, but you are still human. Your body is fragile and breakable, and *that* is why your training is so damned important. You have to want it. You have to strive to be stronger and faster than those dickbags. You have to work out harder than the mercs, train harder than the mercs, and be *smarter* than the mercs. Tactics are key, and when you roll onto a scene and everything is going your way, you don't let your guard down until every last one of those bastards has hit the ground and their breath has left their bodies."

Trenton flexed his muscles and enjoyed the adrenaline running through him.

He was connected to his demon. He could hear the whispered discussions in his mind on how to kill the Damned. They were built-and-booted soldiers, ready to strike the Damned down without remorse.

He and his team were their biggest threat in generations, besides the largest demons.

The difference was that Moloch could create new Enlightened, but large demons were usually lost to the war when they were killed off—at least for the foreseeable future.

The mercenaries knew things were changing, but they had *no* idea what they faced. Trenton knew that.

He was out for blood, blinded by his own thoughts of glory, and determined to be Number One.

General Brushwood looked out the window of his chopper and thought about Colonel Jehovivich.

"Dammit," he growled.

He had worked with her for years, but this was the first time she'd had a solo demon-related mission. He hadn't noticed the way she was before, and to be frank, he wasn't too fond of it. He pulled the mouthpiece of his headset down and spoke to the pilot.

"Can you patch me through to Internal Intelligence? I

need to speak to the head of the department," Brushwood asked.

"Yes, sir," the pilot responded.

The general waited for someone to pick up.

A woman's voice came over the headset. "This is Major Gregory, Internal Intelligence. How may I help you, General?"

"Thank you for taking my call, I was wondering if you would do me a favor," he answered—as if saying no to a general's request for a favor wasn't a career-limiting move. "I have some questions about Colonel Jehovivich that I would like to keep between you and me for the time being."

"Of course, sir. What is your concern?"

"I'm not sure," the general answered, thinking about what his gut was telling him, "but she has recently struck me as being a bit too narrow-minded for the job she has been tasked with. I need to find out if there's something behind it, and if these feelings she has can be changed."

"I can have her file transferred to my desk, General," the major replied. "I will take a thorough look through her history and see if there are any red flags. I know that when you approved her transfer along with yours we didn't do more than a cursory look."

"Understandable," he answered. "And I would appreciate it if you could do that now. If there is a concern, I want to head it off now rather than later. Things are becoming tenser here in this division, and I don't want to question whether I can trust one of my closest advisors."

"Understood," she acknowledged. "We don't want to jeopardize the safety of others for something that could either be fixed or replaced."

"Exactly," the general agreed. "I can wait up to seventy-two hours for the information. I have another crisis on my hands and I won't be able to make a choice on replacing her until that time anyway."

"Perfect, sir," she responded. " I will make sure I brief you personally due to the sensitive nature of your request."

"That is very much appreciated," he told her. "Have a good day."

Brushwood pressed the button on the side of his head-phones and nodded at the pilot.

He turned back toward the window and gazed out again, but there was something unsettled in the pit of his stomach. He had always thought Jehovivich was a bit pushy, but until Katie and the mercenaries had come into the picture she had been agreeable.

There was something about the way she loathed them that was almost unnatural.

Jehovivich pushed her views, overstepped her boundaries, and questioned the general's judgment on a regular basis.

He could deal with strong opinions, but what he could not deal with was someone constantly second-guessing him. He was the general for a reason, and it was really starting to take a toll on him.

Jehovivich might be good at her job, or maybe *had* been good at her job but was starting to frazzle and fizzle.

Their line of duty forced them to be on the top of their games and make hard decisions. He was sure he couldn't trust her to do that.

He sighed. *"Dammit."*

He didn't want to replace the colonel, but if it was that

or dealing with uncertainty—especially in a combat situation—he had no choice but to get rid of her.

He still couldn't believe how fast everything had changed.

The demons were worse than ever, the government was aligned with mercenaries for pretty much the first time in history, and his team was struggling to keep up.

It had gotten to the point where his mood sank every time his phone rang.

Brushwood didn't know when or where the next incursion would hit, but he had begun to accept the idea that a lot more would die before that war was over.

He sighed one last time. "Dammit!"

Charles Butler, the ammunition specialist tasked with helping Korbin's Killers, sat in his temporary office talking to his boss on the phone.

He had one last call to make before he was ready to leave for his new assignment. He had to let his primary company know how long he would be gone and give them whatever detail he could divulge.

Which wasn't very much, considering the secrecy of the mission.

"I am expecting to be offsite for an extended period of time," he explained to his boss. "I'm not even sure I can give you an estimate of how long. As far as the actual mission, there isn't much I can say. I have been instructed by General Brushwood that this operation is under an information-blackout. I won't be able to divulge any information about the mission before, during, or even *after* until the security clearance has been lifted."

"Right. I was part of a mission like this a long time ago," his boss answered. "It's hard sometimes to keep it all to yourself, but if they are labeling it as such I suspect there is a very good reason."

"Well, from the little I was told I understand the blackout," Charles replied. "It's amazing how different the world is sometimes. You learn some crazy shit when you get recruited by the military and read in.. Back when I served it was 'shut up and do as you are told.' Rarely did they give any kind of background or reasoning for their operations." Charles laughed. "I definitely like it better on this side of things."

"Better pay, too." His boss chuckled in agreement.

"That's true," Charles said. "So you aren't upset about the secrecy or the fact that I will be gone so long? If it becomes a problem I hope you will let me know. I can talk to the general."

Loaned to the government or not, he didn't want to lose his job.

"No, no." His boss sounded supportive. "We serve the country. The military is our client and we are here to serve our client, not to get our information-junkie rocks off."

"Absolutely, sir," Charles replied.

His boss continued. "Let me know if you need us to do anything else for you. If anyone gives you shit, throw my name around and you should be able to find just about anything you need. I'll text you my cell number and we will get things accomplished that way."

"Thank you, sir."

"You bet. Be safe out there," his boss replied. "Talk soon."

Charles hung up and sat there perplexed for several moments.

His boss had always been a bit of a hard-ass, and though he allowed his team to be contracted to clients, Charles had figured he would be pissed to lose his services for an undisclosed amount of time with no real explanation.

He wasn't sure why his boss was being so supportive. It seemed out of his character, and frankly a bit suspicious.

Still, Charles was relatively new at the company and had been trying hard to get his boss's attention.

He'd finally gotten it. He told himself to stop dissecting every detail of his reaction, just enjoy finally being part of a team again. He had missed it a lot. Katie seemed to be a bit of a hard-ass, but he knew that she would eventually learn to trust him and allow him to do his job.

These people protected civilians, which was enough to make him want to help.

Though he had no idea what he was walking into, he really was curious to find out about this special metal they had talked about.

Obviously it was something important, since the military had jumped on board and were handing over their civilian contractors to help in the effort. He just hoped he didn't run into any of those rogue demons, whoever they were.

They sounded absolutely terrifying.

9

A s the helicopter came in for a landing, Katie looked out at the ranch.

Cattle grazed in the fields and long stretches of open land and woods backed up to an old farmhouse. It wasn't what she was used to seeing, and it was kind of nice to be somewhere that didn't have sand and rocks as far as the eye could see.

A bit better location than Grains-in-the-Ass, Nevada, Pandora agreed.

You can thank your brother for that, Katie replied. *We had a place closer to Vegas that was nicer.*

Wonderful. You are *talking about Cactus-Spines-in-the-Tits, Nevada, right?*

Katie thought about that. *Not many places that don't have sand or cactus around Vegas.*

Bullshit! I've seen the commercials for Steep Village.

Do what?

Steep Village, on Lake Tahoe.

That's "Incline Village," and yeah, it's beautiful, but it's up in the trees and stuff. What are you going to do about donuts? You wouldn't be near any towns.

What do you call living in Grains-in-the-Ass right now? It isn't like there's a fucking Krispy Kreme next door or anything. Hell, I'd even settle for a Dunking Donuts.

It's Dunkin'.

What's Dunking?

The name of the place is 'Dunkin' Donuts.' There is no 'g.'

Well, it can be dunk-your-stick-in-my-hole donuts for all I care. My point is we don't have them now, so what the fuck do I care if our base is up in the trees? At least we wouldn't be picking sand out of your...

Stop! Katie sighed. *Seriously? Do we have to go through names?*

Like vagina?

Yes!

What about coot box

No.

Silver-Tongued Devil?

There is no silver!

Might be when you get older, Pandora opined. *I've never had my hair go silver, so I couldn't tell you.*

Have you got this off your chest yet, Pandora?

Oh, hell no. I've got dozens. Sure, you have the basics such as coochie, twat, and vulvita maximus. Then we move on to older versions such as Shakespearean words including house, case, pie-corner, porridge, and French weathered pear, although let me tell you that you DON'T want to be called that one.

What the hell? Katie interrupted. *Shakespeare?*

Yeah, nice enough guy, although he sucked in bed. I suggested French weathered pear myself. That's why I know it's a good one.

Are you kidding me?

Perhaps? But probably not. He really was just shit in bed. Of course, then there's altar of Venus, for obvious reasons, continuing with Netherlands—have to say I love that we have a whole country named for our private parts. Is there a country named Penis? I thought not. Moving on, you have phoenix nest, Mrs. Fubbs' parlor, and a personal favorite, lady's low toupee.

That's...kinda funny.

I know, right? There is the beloved road to christening, pink pearl, and then we segue into more erotic versions such as flower, canal, and pool of moisture. A few funny ones...

How many do you know? Katie asked in exasperation. *I bet I don't even know five!*

Well, that was before me. Get into a game of "Name the Sex Organ" on TV and we will sweep it, I promise. Back to me before you interrupted, and we have cock sock, penis glove, and cock pocket. I just love alliteration, very poetic... Cookie nookie, and banana basket.

Holy crap.

I know, right? I got more. Let's go with gross.

Let's not.

You have any donuts?

No.

Chicken nuggets?

No.

Then you are on my time. Gross for $400, Alex: cum dumpster, sperm bottle, cum craver, and the ever-awful goop chute.

Have you had enough? Katie sounded a bit desperate.

No. I've got about another hundred and twenty I think.

Let's save that for a rainy day...say the tenth rainy day in a year?

Yeah, okay... Wait a minute, it almost never rains in the fucking desert!

Sucks to be the person who already agreed.

Bitch!

Thank you.

You have been well-trained.

Learned from the head bitch herself.

I'm so proud. I think I might hurl.

Not inside me.

Yeah, gross. Pandora agreed.

Katie put Pandora's antics out of her mind. She was hoping this incursion wasn't going to turn into an all-out battle, but she didn't really know what to expect.

Everything looked quiet. Even the big white house with the wraparound porch looked peaceful and serene. From experience, though, Katie knew that wasn't a reliable sign. She was just glad there weren't bodies strewn all over the yard.

She glanced at Korbin, who looked concerned, and decided there was no way she could lay it all on him like Pandora wanted her to.

She needed to be able to talk with him calmly, not when they were about to walk into an incursion. That would be a surefire way to distract him, and when someone was distracted they could easily be killed or get others killed.

Katie was determined to walk out of this incursion with no team fatalities, no matter what it took.

The helicopter landed, and they all climbed out and

grabbed their gear. Katie ducked and ran over to Korbin, who stood in the long blowing grasses.

The cows mooed loudly as they scattered through the field, terrified by the helicopter. She didn't blame them. She doubted a helicopter had landed in the field before.

Korbin turned to Katie and Damian.

"We don't have any intel on this, so we need to go in carefully," he yelled over the sound of the chopper. "I am hoping that since everything looks calm this is something small that can be easily taken care of. You two stick together for now. If things change, we will make tactical calls."

Katie nodded. "Got it."

"I'll take the back," Damian told them, pulling out his pistol.

"And I'll take the front." Korbin nodded. "Katie, before we go in, you said you had something to tell me?"

"I'll get with you later on it," she yelled. "Not the time or place."

"All right. Let's move out."

Change your mind? Pandora asked.

It's not the right time, Katie replied. *He isn't going to understand, and walking into an incursion is not the right moment to drop a bomb like that on him. It could get him killed.*

That's fine, Pandora agreed, surprising Katie. *We will talk when we get back. There are other options, and maybe time will help enable you to tell Korbin. I don't like humans or anything, but he seems like a decent level-headed one.*

Yeah. Katie chuckled.

The team hunched as they made their way through the field toward the house.

As they approached the barn they slowed, and as they were about to pass it Korbin raised his fist and pointed at the back of the building.

In the shadows stood a young boy no older than eleven or twelve. He looked scared, and his eyes were big as saucers. Katie nodded and took the lead, knowing that a female presence wouldn't be quite as scary as two grown men approaching.

He's hiding, but he's not possessed, Pandora told her. *Go easy. I can smell his fear from here.*

Got it, Katie replied, turning to Korbin. "Wait here just a second. We don't want to rush the poor kid. He's scared, not possessed."

Korbin and Damian nodded and Katie put her knives into their sheaths and slowly walked forward.

The boy stepped sideways and pressed his shoulder against the barn, clasping his hands in front of him. Katie paused for a moment, then started toward him again. When she reached him she knelt so they were eye to eye.

She looked into his eyes just to double-check and smiled sweetly at him.

"Hi there. My name is Katie. What's yours?"

"Thomas," he said carefully.

"Well, Thomas, it's nice to meet you," she replied. "Are you hiding out here?"

"Yes," he whimpered.

"It's all right," she assured him. "I'm here to help, and those two men behind me—they're here to help too. One of them is a priest. Do you go to church?"

"Yes," he responded. "And Sunday school."

"Good for you." She smiled. "Can you tell me what is happening inside?"

"They're sick," he told her quietly. "I was supposed to get help, but then I got scared and you landed in that big helicopter."

"Yeah, it helped us to get to you as fast as we possibly could," she replied. "It's actually a lot of fun to ride in, you go really fast. So who is inside?"

"My mom and dad," he stated. "And my sister and brother. They're older than me."

"Okay, and are they all sick?"

"No, just my sister and brother. They got sick out of nowhere. My mom and dad aren't sick though, or at least they weren't when they sent me out here."

Katie could only assume that by "sick" he meant they were possessed, and she immediately feared for the safety of the parents. She had no idea how dangerous these demons were, or if they had already done the damage she most feared. This young boy was out here all alone. He reminded her of all the children who had been lost to demons in the past. No matter what happened to his family, she had to make sure he got out of there safely.

"Can you tell me what happened?" Katie asked.

He nodded. "We were just playin' a game, me and my sister and brother. Then out of nowhere Isadora started screaming at the top of her lungs. It was so *loud*! I had to cover my ears with my hands. I turned and there was Benjamin clucking like a chicken, only both of their eyes were tomato-red. My mom and dad grabbed me and told me to get out of the house."

"So that's why you are out here now?"

"Yeah." He shook his head. "My mom and dad have been fighting Isadora and Benjamin, trying to keep them in the house. They told me to get help, so I grabbed my momma's cell phone and called the police."

Thomas handed Katie the cell phone and she looked down at the ended call. Although the boy tried to dial 911, in his panic he had accidentally dialed 666 instead.

Katie shook her head in confusion and looked down at the number again. How the hell did dialing 666 get him an immediate phone connection to the demon-busters?

She knew nerves had caused him to misdial, but good lord, it couldn't have worked out better.

"Okay." Katie handed the phone back to him. "I bet you know a whole lot of places to hide in this barn."

"Yeah."

"I want you to find the best one—the sneakiest one—and stay hidden no matter what," Katie told him. "I want you to stay hidden until I come to get you. When you hear my voice, you will know that it's safe to come out. Can you do that for me?"

"Yep," he agreed, nodding.

"Good! Go ahead, and remember—no matter what you hear, if it's not me calling for you, stay *hidden*."

Thomas nodded and ran into the barn, shutting the big squeaking doors behind him. Katie walked back to the guys and explained exactly what he had said to her. Damian looked at the house and sighed, pulling out his cross.

Slowly they crept to the house and peeked in the windows off the porch. There were four people in the living room and Katie could see the red eyes even from there. The mother and father weren't possessed, but their daughter and son were.

They *were* trying to keep them inside.

Damian nodded and the three entered slowly. Katie stared at the kids, whose demons snarled in anger. She looked at the parents and sighed, shaking her head.

"My name is Katie. We found Thomas and sent him to a safe place, and we are here to help you."

The parents nodded. "Thank you."

Damian slowly walked toward the boy, Benjamin, who growled as thick black goo dripped out of his mouth and down his chin. Damian recited excerpts from his exorcism ritual as he approached, holding his cross up. He took one swipe at Damian, then backed away, screaming and hissing at the cross.

"*A ludum, ludum speculum aliquis stultus. Vocaverunt eos et daemonis nesciunt. Modicum et iam non ego scio quod non reliquit, ut domum palatum parum onto eam moratum atque meam.*"

This one is weak, but not the other, Pandora warned.

Damian grabbed the boy by the shoulder and repeated his words, holding the cross in front of his face. Finally the boy quieted and his eyes rolled into the back of his head.

Damian pushed the demon down farther and farther until he was able to damn the demon back to hell.

The boy fell into Damian's arms and he laid him on the couch, watching the girl the whole time. Isadora jumped onto a table by the wall, where she squatted and watched in excitement as her demon rolled around inside of her.

Damian fought to push the demon out of the girl. It was stubborn and strong, and the more forceful Damian was the angrier the demon got.

Nothing seemed to work, and Damian even went as far as placing the cross on the girl's forearm. Smoke rose from it, but the girl didn't budge. She just glared at him angrily.

This was not going to be as simple as saying lines from the bible and casting it out.

Let me have a go at her, Pandora growled. *The bitch is mine.*

All right, Katie replied. *But I want you to keep her alive. No killing.*

Katie walked over to Korbin, knowing it was time for her to step in.

"I need you to get everyone but Damian, me, and the girl out of this house," Katie told him. "This is a stronger demon, and I don't want bystanders hurt."

"I can do that," Korbin replied.

He lifted the boy off the couch and cradled him in his arms as he turned to the parents.

"Come with me. I'm going to get you to safety."

The mom looked between her son and Damian. "What about our daughter?"

"She will be fine. She is in good hands," Korbin answered, heading toward the door.

He led them out to the yard, closing the door behind him.

Katie cracked her neck back and forth as she prepared herself for Pandora to take over. She needed to help this girl before it was too late. A demon of that size could have easily taken over her mind, body, and soul and left nothing but a body for them to dispose of, but the girl was fighting. That was a good sign.

Hold on tight, Pandora warned. *This won't be pretty.*

Katie groaned softly. She hated it when Pandora took over her vocal cords.

Pandora moved Katie's body toward the girl and put her hand up to Damian. Damian nodded and stepped aside.

Katie opened her mouth, but Pandora took over.

She spoke with authority, her voice deeper than normal. It echoed through every corner of the place and immediately the demon became restless. Katie could sense its fear.

"*Rae, esaeu yorraeq edoes sabbia,*" Pandora began. "*Gae esaeu trael s'ae I oz? I oz ya ziedabbi aem ya knaoq T'Chezz oth I lizz xa zaena yor soddes qae zota zuna esaeu zummabbi ir torture maen or eternity.*"

What language is that? Katie asked.

Mine, Pandora replied. *It's demon.*

Pandora growled louder. "*I oz lizing zes patience, beast.*"

Without warning, the girl started to scream again. She held her ears and fell to her knees. The sound was almost deafening, and it didn't resemble any scream Katie had heard before. The demon pulled itself from the girl's chest and dissipated into thin air. Its face bore an expression of complete horror, as though panicked by the words Pandora had spoken.

The demon went back to hell, too frightened to even try to explain through his human.

He was absolutely terrified of Pandora, which seemed to be a common trend from demon to demon.

You've never spoken this way to any demon before, Katie mused. *I didn't know you'd learned a new language.*

Trust me, it isn't new, Pandora said. *It's been around longer than humans. I just tend to not use it unless it is really serious.*

What did you say to it? Katie asked.

Oh, you know, the whole spiel about it killing the girl and me threatening its life, and that's about it.

Katie stepped forward, catching the girl as she passed out and fell off the table.

Katie considered that not only had Pandora spoken demon, she had done it in a way that was beyond commanding. It was almost frightening how she had pushed that demon around, and Katie wondered how long she had known she could do something like that.

It definitely would have been nice to have had that ability *earlier* in the game.

Damian rushed over and took the girl over to the couch, where he brushed her hair back from her face and searched her eyes. He locked eyes with Katie and nodded, but his face was fearful.

If Katie had never heard anything like that come from Pandora, neither had Damian and it shook him up. Katie couldn't remember Damian ever looking at her like that before. He had always been curious, but not afraid.

At least since the house…

C olonel Jehovivich stood quietly in the lobby of Gibbons Games, the company that produced Mirror, Mirror. She was waiting for the CEO, and had given him five minutes.

She stared around the waiting room at the pictures of happy little girls and boys playing the game. She shook her head, thinking about what could come out of those things and what exactly it did to those happy little faces.

"Colonel," a deep voice in front of her said.

There was a tall chubby man walking toward her with his hand out. His hair was combed to the side, and his lips were dry and pasty. She held back her disgust and shook his hand, trying to stall a bit to see if she could get him to cooperate.

"They tell me you have some questions about our newest game." He smiled. "Come on back to my office. The vice-president is here as well to help answer your inquiries."

"Thank you," Jehovivich replied.

She followed him to his office, where another tall man —this one thin and younger, presumedly the VP—waited. The CEO sat down behind his desk and motioned to the chair, but the colonel shook her head politely.

"What can we help you with?"

"I want to find out the history behind your Mirror Mirror game," she said, cutting right to the chase.

"Well, we bought the rights from some academic fellow," he replied. "He told us he made it up, but that it was based on historical documents he had found during an excavation that dated back to the 1600s."

"Have *you* played the game?"

"Of course." He smiled. "Several of us have, and we have had rave reviews on it. It's fun to play with friends. Old and young alike love it, and there are special made-up incantations in the instruction manual. Our VP actually was very hands-on with this one."

Jehovivich continued, "And what is the premise of this game?"

"It is said you can contact the dead, and use the spells to have them do things," he replied. "You have to speak an old language to bespell the opponents back to the dungeon."

"I'm going to make this short and sweet," the colonel said. "We need you to immediately stop production and sales of this product and recall whatever you can from the companies you have sold it to."

"Uh, that's an interesting request." He chuckled. "May I ask why?"

"That information is classified," she said with a straight face.

"Classified...right. A classified shutdown of a children's game. Well, I will need a court order before I'll pull anything."

The colonel's phone rang; it was the general. "Excuse me, it's the boss."

She picked up the phone and walked to the back of the room. She talked quietly, yet still loud enough for the CEO and VP to hear what she was saying. She wanted them to understand she was not there to play games.

"Yes, sir, the game was created based on a swath of papers and documents from hundreds of years ago," she repeated.

"And what did they say about pulling the game?" Brushwood asked.

"They are stating that they will require a court order to stop production or distribution," she replied. "They are not taking me seriously in the least."

"We can't let this continue," Brushwood growled. "They must consent to stop the game immediately or I am afraid we are going to have a rash of new demons spawning, only this time they will be an army of children."

"Understood sir, though I can't really come out and tell them that," she replied.

"You can be rather persuasive when you want to be. I trust that you will come up with the perfect solution for this issue. They don't want to lose money, and they don't understand that they could lose their lives too."

"No, they don't seem to get the seriousness of it, sir," she replied.

"Do whatever you need to, and if I have to get

involved, let me know, I will fly right out there and let them know who is controlling things," Brushwood told her.

"Can I just pull my weapon under the operational guidelines of our mission?"

As Jehovivich said that she looked at the CEO. His eyes were nervous and he licked his dry lips and glanced at the VP. The vice-president put his hand up, shook his head, and tried to calm the president down.

He didn't think there was any way that she could do that, but then again, the world was a little bit different than it used to be.

The colonel hid a smirk and glanced at the VP as he took off his glasses and rubbed the crease in his nose. As he looked up a red ring flashed in the light and Jehovivich quickly dropped her phone, pulled her pistol, and pointed it at the VP.

The president gasped. Other office personnel had stopped in the doorway when they noticed her weapon. She steadied her hand and circled toward the door, keeping her gun pointed at the vice-president's head.

She should have known that someone close to the president or even the president himself was in on this kind of conspiracy.

The words weren't fake at all, and the vice-president knew it. He had inserted incantations into a children's game to create the perfect scenario for demons to infect them.

The vice-president leaned against the wall with a smirk and arrogantly crossed his ankles. He wasn't about to let this go, even if it meant a full-on fight.

Jehovivich could tell he was cocky, but she couldn't tell if that trait belonged to the human or his demon.

Probably a bit of both.

Either way, she now knew that not only was there a demon behind the creation, the game was a real and sincere threat—one that needed to be taken care of before things got any worse. First, though, she needed to take care of the demon in front of her.

"This is absolutely insane," the CEO cried, standing up in a huff. "You can't just walk into our office and demand things. And then you pull a gun? What kind of mission are you on?"

"Shut up," Jehovivich commanded. "And sit the fuck down."

A deep demon laugh blew through the room, surprising the CEO and the gaggle of onlookers. The voice no longer belonged to the VP; it was that of his demon. The CEO plopped down in his chair and gaped at the man in disbelief. The colonel continued to aim her gun at his head.

"You stupid bitch," the demon growled. "I am going to eat you alive. First, though, I am going to hang you upside down, strip you, and run my bladed fingernails down your body. I will make sure you stay alive long enough to feel every inch of pain. Only when I think you have had enough will I stop."

"Uh, you *do* realize that I am holding a gun and you are holding a fountain pen?" the colonel asked.

"That pathetic piece of metal?" The demon laughed. "It is barely strong enough to penetrate my first layer. You think that you can scare me with that." He jerked a thumb at the door. "Get the fuck out of here. You and your general can forget about the *bigger* game. It isn't going anywhere, and the game is key to our world's revival. I can tell you right now, though—if *that* is what you are bringing to the party I have already accomplished my goal, sweet cheeks."

The colonel smirked and pulled the trigger, shooting him right between the eyes. The demon dropped to the floor, screaming in pain as his hands covered his forehead.

She smiled down at her gun—which held the special bullets—and walked toward him. He grumbled, groaned, and cursed.

His face was a bit worse for wear and blood pulsed out of the wound with his heartbeat.

"You *tricky fucking human*," he spat, his eyes red and his voice guttural. "You will pay for this, *bitch!* I will kill you and string your intestines out like a clothesline for all your little friends to lick while I stab them in the ass with a pipe."

The colonel glanced at the crowd, who shook in fear and chattered loudly to each other as the demon sat back up despite his partially-caved-in head.

"You've had your time to speak," she stated. "Got anything else to say, you rotting piece of filth?"

It was doing everything it could to not get sent back to hell, but the colonel just wasn't having it. "You made it possible for a demon from your disgusting dimension to enter a young girl."

"*Bitch!*" he screamed, his strength draining along with his blood because of the metal lodged in his brain.

"You are the scum here on Earth. The worst human is above *you*."

She kicked him in the chest, shoving the demon back to the floor. He hissed but didn't try to get up.

He was too injured at that point, but not enough to just die.

It was at this moment that the colonel realized how much joy she felt. She had the power to get rid of the demon.

She was there alone; no need to answer to the general or anyone else. It was on her to make the choices, and in this scenario?

Killing that bastard was at the top of her list.

"You should lie down. That's quite the bump on the noggin," she told him as she straddled him.

"I'll kill you," he hissed, glaring at her.

She shook her head and spoke without inflection. "I'm gonna say you probably won't."

He gasped and his eyes narrowed. "One day I will find you and I will *kill everyone you love*," he growled, the blood still squirting from the gaping wound.

"This conversation bores me." She leaned forward just a small bit, placing the pistol on his skull. *"Back to hell with you,"* she declared and her pistol bucked twice more, sending two more of the special bullets into his head.

He writhed and groaned as more black blood seeped from the wounds in his skull.

The colonel yawned and waited until the human took his last breath, sending the demon straight back to hell.

She nodded, stood up, and brushed off her hands. The CEO was staring wide-eyed at her and she lifted an eyebrow, waiting for his response. The body behind her shattered into dust.

"I...uh... Okay, no problem," the CEO stuttered and picked up the phone with shaking hands. "I am recalling the games right now."

The general nodded. "I understand. Good job, Colonel. See you back here."

He hung up, then dialed a much longer phone number and waited for the liaison on the other end to pick up. Four phone rings later he got a person.

Normally it was one ring.

"There has been a serious breach in safety protocol in the US." The general got right to the point. "I need to speak to the Chairperson of the Coalition for Neutralization of Alien and Humanity Integration."

The general took a deep breath and sat back in his chair. He couldn't believe that something like this bullshit with a stupid game had gotten so out of hand. What the hell were the demons going to dream up next?

When the head of CNAHI—a horrible acronym if there ever was one—got on the phone, Brushwood straightened.

"This is the Chairperson," was the only greeting.

"This is Brushwood in the US. I want to inform you of a new tactic the demons are using to bring their race over," he told the person. "It is in the form of a children's game, created by some guy who got the idea from some 1600s documents. The game is called Mirror Mirror, and it's incredibly hazardous to the innocent. We've started the process of pulling all merchandise off the shelves here in the States, but some of those games are still in the wild here and abroad, which means we need to make sure all countries pull together in this effort. It is a difficult task, that's for sure, but the game could be a huge contributor to the growing demon population if we aren't careful."

"Understood, General. You will send the relevant information via secure digital means?"

"Yes, already sent. Someone needs to review and get on it ASAP. We've confirmed that the company here in the States had an embedded demon making it happen."

"We will. One moment." There was a noise and muffled words in another language—Russian, he thought—and the voice returned. "We are working on this now. We are tracking an increase of thirty percent in demon incursions in the last thirty-six hours."

"Dammit."

"I agree," the man stated. "If you are a praying man, General, send some of those prayers to Europe, because they need it. I'm afraid we don't have containment on this anymore."

"I haven't been praying," General Brushwood answered, "but I might be soon. If I take it up I'll send you some."

"Thank you."

Each hung up.

The second phone call went to SOCOM, the Special Operations Command group which assigned the general's black ops their missions. His task was pretty specific.

Stop the goddamned demons from infiltrating his area of operations, which presently was the United States—except he had constraints against the amount of firepower he could bring down inside the US.

The line was picked up.

The general spoke with SOCOM, giving them all the details and the main distributor and creator addresses, and tried to tie up as many loose ends as possible.

When he was done he hung up the phone and swiveled his chair toward the window, rubbing his chin. He just didn't understand how a cock-up of those proportions could have possibly happened.

It sounded like the VP had been a demon a lot longer than the game had been out, and had actually had a part in its creation.

How they had missed the production of the game he didn't understand.

The demons had been vicious for a very long time, sure, but smart? They had never mastered smart before.

The good guys needed to find out whether this was an accident or something done on purpose.

Had someone asked him months before if he thought something on that scale could ever be carried out by the demons, he would have laughed the questioner into the ground.

Now, though, he was starting to question their evolutionary traits. They were getting smarter and bigger, and they were certainly much better trained.

The war had just escalated.

The music thumped loudly inside the space as the candles flickered and the alcohol flowed.

The Enlightened had enjoyed a visit from their leader,

Moloch, and he'd told them what their next mission would be.

They were going after a small weapons depot in Washington state. Apparently it was an incredibly important task to widen the war's front.

"To the next round of ass-kickings," one of them toasted, lifting his glass. "May your claws strike true, your dark hearts beat as one, and if killed, may your soul travel quickly to the underworld."

"Hear, hear," the group cheered and downed their drinks.

Moloch's arrival had been fortuitous.

It had renewed their faith, taken away their fears, and made them want to run head-first into a blazing battle to fight for the survival of their chosen masters—the demon race.

Of course, part of what they didn't know was while Moloch pumped them for war, there was a shadow on the sidelines—one that waited for the day the Enlightened were no longer needed and could be disposed of *properly*.

The leader of the group stood watching, not participating but understanding that even though he had calmed them before, it was important for them to be able to let loose now.

They were ready to rock and roll, and as they drank the connection between them and their internal demons grew stronger.

One could feel the waves of power erupting from them. It wasn't about the human contact, it was about the *demon* one, and this was one strong group of people.

Perhaps strong enough to overpower the prepared.

I t had been a long couple of weeks for Katie and she wanted a break, but with the government guys coming to meet Joshua there wasn't *time* for her to get any kind of rest.

She woke up and tried to get Pandora talking.

Katie's conversation went like this:

I'm tired.

Pandora grumped, *Go back to sleep.*

Grouch.

Bitch.

And that was the end.

Katie made her way over to Joshua's area of the base and went inside. She found him working on a new weapon.

"Hey." He smiled and moved from his workbench, giving her a hug. He stepped back to look at her face. "You look tired."

"Yeah, it's been a long few weeks," she admitted.

"Did you get to use the staff yet?"

"No. The last call didn't warrant it, so I've just been practicing," she griped. "But don't worry—with everything going on, I'm sure that I'll get to use it soon."

He shrugged. "What can I do for you this morning?"

"I…" She put a hand over her mouth to cover a yawn. "I came by to get an update before the new guys come in later this morning," she replied, following him over to a nearby couch. "Are you ready for them?"

"I'm not really sure what I should *do* to be ready for them." He snorted and scratched the back of his head. "I mean, I'm assuming they will tell me what they need from me."

"They will." She nodded. "Are you okay working with the metallurgist? I know this stuff is pretty hush-hush; family secret and all that."

He took a deep breath before he answered her. "I think so? Though I am a little nervous about what I can say and can't say."

"Don't be nervous about that. You don't have to talk about the mystery magic side of things if you don't want to," Katie assured him. "I've handled the income issues, and the legal side as well. They've signed contracts, and the government will be absorbing the cost of them being here. All you have to do is work *with* them. I have met both of them, and though they are your typical civilian stuffed shirts, they are pretty nice when they let go just a bit. Both are going to be here for a long time, so it's important to me that they learn how things work; how the rank and file system goes here. They aren't in charge of anything. They are just here to build us a shop—something more efficient that will help you get some rest from time to time and increase production."

"Got it," he declared, nodding like he was mentally taking notes. "Then I'm good. Happy to see what I can learn from these guys, and I'm sure I will be able to teach them a thing or two."

"Perfect." Katie sighed. "Though I have to admit they don't seem like the kind of guys who will be ready and willing to learn anything. They are robots. They pretty much roll in and create spaces and production flows and stuff."

"That's fine with me," Joshua replied. "Honestly, Katie, I am pretty excited to learn more about the metallurgy. I grew up learning everything there was to know about the mystery side of it, but no one ever really took the time to teach me about metals and how they interact and such. I've learned some from books, but I think it will help me with my weapons-smithing. If I know how to handle a metal I can practically do anything with it."

Katie felt a load drop off of her chest. "Good. I was really hoping that you wouldn't be nervous about this change," she admitted. "Now, all that said, you can't give away too much information. There are things that even *I* don't know. It should be your general rule of thumb that if *I* don't know something, they shouldn't either. At the same time, we desperately *need* to make this all work. There aren't enough mercenaries to tackle the influx of demons as it is, and these weapons are one answer to that shortage."

Joshua nodded, lost in thought for a moment. "Do you think you will be bringing in new people? For our team?"

"Eventually. But with the other teams missing so many

men and us only missing one, we might stay at six for quite a while, which leaves us at a disadvantage," Katie explained. "Amy's team is down to three functional members right now. They're backstopping with redshirts, so they are pretty much in a holding pattern until their men recover or they are given some new people." She put a hand on his arm. "Using these bullets made with your metal is like having another person on the team; we can take down twice as many demons. It allows the normal humans to play in this game as well."

"Okay, boss." Joshua grabbed a red cotton rag that was hanging out of a pocket and used it to dry his hands. "Weapons are the answer, so I'll make this work as well as I can."

"If you need me to, I'll come down and work with you guys," she told him. "Just give me a ring. I'd like to touch base with them when they get here anyway, since they are new and will need to get used to the way we do things."

"I'll make sure to text you when they arrive or call the desk and tell Stephanie in case you're in the tunnels." He glanced at her. "Will that work?"

"Yes, and thank you, Joshua." Katie smiled and stood up. "I guess I better get some breakfast in me and then head over to get some training in before they arrive. I'm really hoping to get a chance to try out my new staff on the next operation, but we will see. On the one hand I want to use it, but on the other it would mean that there is an incursion, which pretty much sucks ass."

Joshua chuckled. "We live double-edged lives. But I am sure you will like it, and hopefully when this new setup is completed I will be able to start working on cooler weapons; things we haven't used before."

"You are the best, sir." Katie smiled.

She headed out of his building toward her breakfast. Joshua and his family secrets needed to stay hidden, even with the new guys coming. Somehow they had to make certain of that.

Because for the demons, he was a prime target.

———

"Swing low," the commander called. "You want to hit them in the knees to take them down. Then swing up and over, pushing the sword, staff, knife—whatever—deep into their chest. The metal is going to stun them, so even if that blow doesn't kill you will have time to shoot them, set them on fire, or whatever you need to do to kill the sonsabitches."

The Special Operation, Small Tac Team, was in the government training facility working with one of the new instructors. They worked on hand-to-hand combat as well as they possibly could.

The leader walked through, studied the men's practice, shifted stances, gave demonstrations, and watched as the men began to get better.

Sure, they didn't have the power of a Damned, being "innocents," but they had pushed their bodies to the limit and kept on going. As he approached the front of the room to start a new string of moves, the alarm went off and those in the group prepared to head to their posts.

A young soldier ran into the room and handed the

trainer a piece of paper with instructions from the general on them. He read it, then addressed the men.

"All right, men, the demon attack is located one hour east at an armory," he yelled. "Gear up, grab your weapons, and let's hit the helicopter pad!"

The men were ready in five minutes and in the air within ten.

They landed outside the perimeter of the armory in an open area. The men lined up with the leader and slowly crept toward the building, watching for signs of demons. Everything seemed relatively quiet, but that could be a trick.

There had been many changes in the recent weeks, so these men didn't put anything by the new breed of demon.

The leader led them in cautiously and slowly. They entered the outer layer of the building, standing quietly behind one another. When they reached the main space, they found several demons wreaking havoc.

They were there for the weapons or the intel and gave no real signs of cooperating.

"GO!"

As before they started to plow through the demons, fighting hard and fast and feeling the energy that came from winning.

"DAN!" Jeff called. "Upside!"

Dan, who was on the floor, rolled to his left. He aimed up and shot three times into the demon trying to drop in on him.

Dust caked his face.

It had been a long time since they had gone into an incursion and everyone had come back out.

"They taste like chicken." He spat out the dust. "Very dehydrated chicken, but chicken."

The chuckles on the line gave way to the command to "keep your focus."

"Whoop!" Fists went up in the air.

Jeff, their lead, began to clap but stopped quickly as the main door flew open and a group of Damned walked in. They were dressed in tactical gear and their red eyes shone.

Jeff stared at them. "What team are you with? And why the hell did the general call you in?"

The mercs' leader walked up to him, smiling like he owned the place.

Jeff fucking hated the Damned sometime. Cocky sons-abitches.

"Let me try this again, perhaps a little slower. What. Are. You. Doing. Here?" He smiled and gestured behind him. "We didn't call any of the mercenaries out, and we already got them all. No money for you here."

The mercs' leader leaned in, waving Jeff a little closer. "We are here," he licked his lips, one hand casually resting on his knife handle as he whispered, "because *we aren't on your side*." Trenton smiled.

"What? We just..."

Jeff froze, then looked at his stomach.

"Name's Trenton, by the way."

Jeff coughed, spraying Trenton's face with blood, and grabbed the sword in his gut. Trenton yanked the sword out and watched as Jeff's body crumpled to the floor. There was complete silence for half a moment—the kind that is barely measurable, but if you asked those who were there, they would *swear* it had been minutes long.

Battle cries erupted from both groups.

The Enlightened released the demons inside them and fired at the soldiers. A few took hits to their flak jackets, and one got his ear shot off.

One by one the human team were shot down, although a few were killed by machetes and two by Trenton himself.

By the time the ambush was complete, the Enlightened had killed the entire tac team. They stared around the armory.

They had come for the weapons and they weren't leaving without them.

"You two," Trenton called, pointing at two of the Enlightened. "Grab the duffel bags and start filling them."

"Why aren't there more weapons?" Wilson asked from the doorway. "There should seriously be more weapons here." He looked around.

They had hit an armory, but not just any armory—a National Guard Armory. There were a few guns and some other weapons to play with, so they would pack what was there and load it into the cars they had hidden out back.

"Seriously, we could have hit a gun store and had more luck than this," Wilson continued, shoving a grenade in his pocket. "Don't get me wrong; I'm glad we found weapons and everything, but I hate it when we waste our time."

"We took down an entire Special Operations team and you are bitching because we didn't get enough guns?" Trenton asked. "The enemy has…"

Trenton looked down to see he had kicked a disembodied head and lobbed it out of his path.

"Sorry, sir." Wilson watched the head bounce off a wall a couple of feet away. "I apologize."

Trenton waved a hand. "Just do the job. I'm sure things will get a bit more exciting in the days to come."

"Also, about the gun shop," Terence interjected. "Those are civilians, and we could have easily hit a fellow survivalist by mistake. We don't want to do that; it would royally suck."

Trenton shook his head. "Terence, you need to get that pack mentality out of your head and remember— survivalist or not, if they get in *our* way? We handle it," Trenton told him grabbing the full bag from him and throwing it over his shoulder.

Terence nodded, "Got it."

"How are things going with the new guys?" Calvin asked. He and Korbin were sitting at the table eating.

"I think they just got here a little while ago. We're trying to give them some space and time with Joshua," he answered.

"Is that smart?" Calvin asked. "To leave them alone with him?"

"*I* don't like it," Korbin replied. "But at the same time, we agreed to have them here to help. They are going to be here for a while, so we'll have to work on trusting them. The first time they fuck up though...that's when I'll step in and let them know who's boss—which is everyone except them."

"I feel bad for Joshua. You know how nervous he gets

around people." Calvin took a bite of his sandwich. "Wish we had Pringles."

"Add it to the grocery list," Korbin suggested. "But yeah, he has gotten a lot more confident lately. These guys are regulars. They are there basically to work with and for Joshua. He knows that, so I think he will be fine with it all."

"How are you and Stephanie doing?"

"Oh, is that how it goes?" Korbin laughed loudly. "We're talking about government help, and then oops! We roll right into my love life."

"Sorry, man." He laughed. "I just saw Miss Stephanie covered in donuts talking about a forgive-me gift once upon a time. I never got to ask what happened with Part Two."

"Oh, yeah." Korbin grunted. "Forgot about that. I guess I'm just still getting used to the idea of having a woman in my life again. It's a slow process for me."

"Understandable." Calvin smiled. "I think you deserve it, though. You've sacrificed for everyone else for so long that I think it's about time you do it for yourself. Have a little happiness in your life."

"I'll be happy when we stop talking about my love life." Korbin chuckled and pulled his beeping phone from his pocket.

Calvin watched Korbin's face as he read the email. It went from a sunny smile deep into the shadows of anguish.

Calvin shifted in his chair and took another bite of his sandwich. He got uneasy when Korbin was upset. He had seen that face before, so he knew that it wasn't anything good.

"What's going on?" Calvin asked.

"Apparently there was a government raid in Washington State last night," Korbin explained. "It was a National Guard Armory. All the government soldiers died." Korbin looked up. "There wasn't one single survivor."

"What happened?" Calvin said, his heart beating fast.

"I don't know for sure. It doesn't say." Korbin looked back down. "Hopefully I can get some answers when I call in later, but I'll tell you what—this does not have normal demon raid written on it."

"I don't know," Calvin argued. "I wouldn't jump to conclusions. I've seen those guys fight, and a big incursion could have done the trick."

"Yeah." Korbin exhaled and put his phone on the table. "But a mercenary demon group could also have rolled in and killed everyone. We know they are on the loose, so now comes the job of finding those fuckers."

K atie gripped her truck's steering wheel as she plowed through the sand toward the mountains at the back of the property.

She hadn't been out there since she'd spread Derek's ashes, and although it was hard for her, she knew that she needed to just do it.

She hit the gas harder, cresting a ridge and going airborne for a moment. When she crashed back down she smiled, thinking about the time she and Derek had run wild through that very desert.

It was one of her best memories; something she would hold onto for a very long time.

When Katie reached the mountain, she didn't head up in the truck.

Instead she parked at the base, deciding she could use the exercise.

She got out, grabbed her bag, threw it on her back, and

stretched her arms into the air. The morning was beautiful and the sun was just coming over the horizon.

Katie had made sure to leave before anyone else was awake or mainlining caffeine. She needed some time to herself. She started up the mountain and felt the burn in her thighs and calves as she climbed.

Pandora didn't juice her, but instead stayed quiet, letting her get in the cardio she wanted.

When she reached the flat area where Derek's ashes had been spread, she stopped and knelt to run her hand across the sand. She still couldn't believe he was gone. She remembered all the times she'd find him waiting for her, holding out his phone to show her some stupid meme.

She sighed and stood up, looking out over the desert. It was beautiful up here. If she'd had the time she could stand there all day, but that wasn't what she had come there to do.

Katie had come there to practice with her new weapon. She had played around in the training area, but with the blades being special metal she didn't want to accidentally hurt anyone so she'd held back, not really able to give it her all.

Out here on the mountain plateau in the quiet of the desert morning, she would be able to concentrate; really open up to Pandora and just let things *go* for a while.

Just fucking *go.*

She had this amazing weapon, but one didn't just run into a building swinging something like her new staff around at her leisure. You had to be in control, to have it move *with* your body, not have your body move it.

Pandora knew a lot about it too, and she was ready to

school Katie on the correct body stances and moves she would need to master her new quarterstaff.

You there? Katie asked.

I am, Pandora replied. *Just waiting on you.*

Katie pulled out both pieces and locked them together, tossing her bag to the side. She placed herself in a starting stance and rotated her body, slicing the staff through the air. She stood up straight and did it again, this time moving her feet farther.

That's good, Pandora told her, b*ut you are still fighting it. You need to relax and make the staff an extension of your body. You need to—and I know this sounds corny—become one with the weapon.*

It's hard. It feels so strange, and I know what is in it, Katie explained.

Why don't you let me show you?

Katie took a deep breath and allowed Pandora to inhabit her whole body.

She could still feel the movement of her muscles and the way the wind blew across her face—and exactly how hard she needed to grip the staff.

Pandora moved her through the motions, showing her the stances, the way that the staff was designed to cut through the air, and how to push with maximum force. Once Katie's body was rolling through the motions like they were natural, Pandora amped up her speed and skill.

Katie twisted and pulled the staff apart.

She whirled quickly and sliced the sticks through the air, then whipped them back to her sides. She jumped and kicked her legs out, slamming the tip of the staff into the dirt as if she were striking an opponent on the ground in the chest.

She knelt for a moment as Pandora gave her time to catch her breath.

That's unreal, Katie exclaimed. *No one sees fighting like that anymore. No one has the discipline to learn how to do that.*

You're right, Pandora admitted. *Practice isn't the same as it was when we did it thousands of years ago. Then there was nothing but you and your weapon. Everyone gets so comfortable now in the fact that they have guns and crazy knives, and other things that make being a lazy fighter much easier. When you have nothing but you and a wooden pole you learn to use that pole the best way you can. You learn to be disciplined. You learn that your health, your physique, and your strength play more of a role in fighting than the weapon itself does. Eventually you learn that your mind is really the controlling factor.*

I can see that, Katie agreed, walking over to her bag and grabbing a bottle of water.

Think about how you felt when you first got here, waving the pole through the air and trying to find your steps. You were timid, but once you let your mind go—once you were confident in your grip, and trusted in me—you were unstoppable. It all connects, and it is much more than just aim-and-shoot. That is why you will survive long after the others—because your mind is there.

Katie sat down on a rock and sipped her water, letting the breeze hit her sweaty cheeks and forehead. It cooled her, and she loved the way it felt.

Pandora had been serious all morning. She wasn't used to that, but she figured that since she had her in that mood she might as well take advantage of it. She had been thinking a lot lately, and Katie, though most of the time she ignored it, had taken notice.

It was hard not to notice when your loud friend suddenly grew quiet.

So, what's been on your mind lately? Katie asked. *You've been really quiet and contemplative.*

Honestly? Pandora said. *I've been thinking about getting a divorce.*

Katie choked on her water. *Wait, what? From who? I didn't know you were married.*

Yeah, I've been married for a long time, she admitted. *It's not love, really. It was a marriage of convenience more than anything. He's a complete asswipe, and it's not like he doesn't have at least a dozen or more concubines. It just so happens that I am the biggest bitch of all.*

That's not hard to believe. Katie giggled. *Where did you meet him?*

Friend. Which should explain everything.

Do I know him? I mean, have we met him?

Yeahhhh, I don't think so. Pandora chuckled. *I would have noticed if we had, I think. To be honest, he is a monumental asshole. There is really no one worse. He even outshines my PITA brother, and to do that is a serious feat.*

So you've been thinking about that this whole time? Katie asked. *You could have talked to me about it. Not that I've had much experience with that kind of thing, but I could have given you some sisterly solidarity. You know, agreed with you on everything, called him a douchebag a few times, and plotted his death with you.*

That sounds nice. Pandora laughed. *But to be honest, that's not the only thing that's been on my mind. I've also been thinking about my future. It's all a lot of nothing since we will probably die together soon, but hey...a girl can dream.*

I hope we don't *die soon,* Katie ground out. *That's why I am out here mastering my tools with you.*

You need to master some other tools too, Pandora told her. *If you know what I mean.*

Katie laughed and shook her head, noticing that she had changed the subject and gotten feisty again. She wanted to ask what she thought about her future, but she didn't want to push it—not when Pandora had made the effort to say that much.

Katie took another sip of water, acknowledging what a big deal it was that Pandora had spoken with her. Normally, she didn't open up at all to Katie, unless of course it had to do with food or sex. Still, it was a good start.

So let me ask you this...what could you do with me if I trusted you completely? Katie asked.

Pandora didn't answer for a moment, and Katie looked out over the desert. It was coming to life as the sun hit it.

Why don't we find out?

Two Weeks Later

The base had been so quiet. Two weeks had gone by with not a single call. It was practically unheard of, especially in that long a period of time.

On one hand the teams needed the break, but on the other hand they were incredibly wary about what the hell the demons were doing out there.

Stephanie had offered to chase some down, but Korbin had said no. They would need the rest and he wanted them to train more if they were going to walk into something big soon.

They didn't need to be running all over putting themselves at risk. Things were different now, mostly because of the new demon merc team that snuck around and took down anyone they could.

This new team concerned Korbin. He knew they were good, and he knew they were getting stronger by the day.

What he *didn't* know was where they were and who the hell was running the operation. The last thing he wanted was to find himself unprepared and have his team face a squad that harnessed powers his team did not.

These survivalists had a leader training them; his side just hadn't nailed the details down quite yet.

So for two weeks the team spent their time finishing up little odds and ends around the base, training if they weren't sleeping, and enjoying their evenings off together.

It was almost like old times, but there was an air of caution floating around; one that made your skin crawl if you really thought about it.

It was early afternoon and training was complete. Eric was at the table eating his lunch and listening to the radio.

He jammed to the music, not paying much attention to anything going on in the world or on the base, for that matter.

When the song stopped and the commercials started he almost turned it off, but he paused when he heard an announcement for donuts. A local radio station was putting on a donut-eating contest in Las Vegas and the prizes were awesome, but even more awesome was the prospect of free donuts for the *next year*.

That sounded like it was right up Katie's and Pandora's alley.

He jumped up and made his way through the tunnels to Katie's room, but when he knocked there was no answer so he turned to leave.

"Lookin' for me?" she asked as she came up.

"Yes," Eric exclaimed excitedly, his eyes alight. "I just heard the single most awesome thing ever on the radio."

Katie looked at him funny, wondering what the joke was. "Prince came back to life?"

Eric shook his head. "No, but that would be awesome too." He smiled. "A donut shop in Las Vegas is having a donut-eating contest and it's being sponsored by a local radio station. It is right up our alley, so I think we should stop being so serious and go sign up for it."

"I don't know." Katie bit her lip.

Do it, bitch! Pandora urged. *It's my dream come true.*

After dinner, Katie wandered to the surface and headed over to Joshua's place.

Charles and Travis had been there with Joshua for over two weeks now, and she was ready for her next update.

Joshua had taken to them pretty quickly, liking their no-nonsense talk and the way they carried themselves. He had said they reminded him of his father when he was young. Very straight and narrow, never bending, and serious. *Dead* serious about his work.

Over the past two weeks they had moved most of Joshua's furnishings and a bunch of new machines had been set up. It looked like a factory, that was for sure, but those machines were going to make the magic happen.

It was nice looking at her company and feeling a sense of pride. She was actually pretty happy Brushwood had helped them, even if it was because he needed the rounds. She would have never been able to come up with stuff like this on her own.

"Hey," Joshua called, waving.

"Hey, guys," Katie said walking over to the machine they were looking at. "How is everything going?"

"Good," Travis told her, smiling for the first time that Katie had seen.

"Really good," Charles added. "This is a fun project."

"Good." She laughed.

"So we were just talking about how we need a chunk of the metal, specifically a forty-pound ingot, to which we will apply two-hundred-and-fifty-tons of pressure to push it into a wire. That will be used to build the rounds."

Katie just blinked at Joshua.

"I know that sounds kind of…."

"Boring?" Katie suggested, looking at Joshua.

"I was going to say complicated, but that works."

"So what it ultimately has done," Charles explained, walking her through the machines, "is allow us to now make multiple sizes. Whatever the gun, we can most likely make a round for it now. Shotgun shells are a bit different —although in some ways easier, since they can be pellets or flechettes—but any of the others, we got you on lockdown."

"I was thinking we would end up going to a .45 hollow point," Joshua offered.

Katie shrugged. "Hey, whatever we need we need. I trust your judgment, Joshua, and you know what kind of guns we have."

"I do, and I'm going to do another inventory in a couple days and write down all the different sizes we need to make. We will replace the old rounds with the new, and with all the machines we can produce them so fast we might not use them all."

"If we keep having radio silence like this, that's likely." Katie sighed.

"Things quiet down there?" Charles asked.

"Yeah, a little too quiet." Katie looked around before turning back to the guys. "Something is stirring and we will find out right after it bites us on the ass, I think."

J oshua shuffled through some papers on his desk, trying to find the formula he had written down.

The shop was louder than normal, but Joshua didn't mind. The girls were back, and they were trying to get the place straightened up. There was a lot of work to do now that the machines were there, and Joshua knew he was going to need all the help he could get.

Besides, he was tired of working with the government guys; he missed the way things had been. Just like when they moved to the base, Joshua felt uneasy. He wasn't very good with change.

One of the girls walked over and handed Joshua a grape soda, his favorite. He smiled and nodded, sitting down and taking a sip as she walked away.

Charles and Travis looked at each other and back at Joshua. He knew they were standing there—and why—but he wasn't about to turn around and look at them. It was the first time they had met the staff, and Joshua could almost smell the desperation seeping from them both. It was comical, but at the same time he knew they'd better watch themselves. These girls weren't like normal females in town.

"Joshua," Travis whispered, "when you said 'staff' we didn't realize you meant all the hot women in Las Vegas."

"Yeah, man." Charles chuckled. "How do you get any work done around here?"

"They are good people." Joshua put down his pen and turned his chair toward them. "These girls were in a different profession before they came here, if you catch my drift."

"Really?" Travis smiled as one of them walked past.

"Yeah," Joshua replied. "But don't underestimate these girls. They are not easy pickings. These women faced demons head-on and didn't run away. They shoved their knives straight into their bellies and watched them turn to dust."

"Whoa." Travis' eyes opened wide and flicked to the girls and back.

"I don't imagine they would have much of a problem taking a blade to an asshole if said asshole was being rude." Joshua smirked. "Just like Katie, these women are tough as nails. They are pretty on the outside—and pretty on the inside—but all of that is wrapped up in a steel cage. These days they'd rather kick your ass than deal with your shit, so disrespect is completely off the table." He waffled for a moment. "If you want to keep your nuts, that is."

"We wouldn't even think about disrespecting them." Charles shook his head, eyes wide.

"Nope, not a single thought of disrespect going through

my mind," Travis agreed. "In fact, I think I will just get back to work."

"Me too." Charles pushed Travis back out onto the floor.

Joshua looked down at his papers again and smiled. He was going to protect those girls no matter what, even if it took fear to do so. By the looks of it, he had done more than enough to instill that fear.

***

Korbin passed the plate of pancakes across the table to Stephanie, who snuck him an intimate glance and winked.

Korbin tried to hold back a smile and looked down, clearing his throat. Damian read the paper as always, sipping his coffee and carefully eating his three pieces of perfectly-prepared cinnamon and sugar toast.

Calvin was in his own world, buttering his gigantic stack of flapjacks and staring at the huge bottle of real maple syrup in the center of the table. He had gotten up early and cooked breakfast and, figuring everyone would be hungry, he had made more than enough for three teams.

Mornings were usually chaotic for the team, no one really eating breakfast unless it was an apple or a granola bar they grabbed on the way to the training room. Coffee was usually the beverage of choice for everyone, but it was the weekend and Calvin liked it when everyone ate together. It was as close to a family situation as they could get.

He might understand that he would never have the wife, kids, and backyard barbeque, but he was determined to make something more out of the situation they were in than just killing demons and taking names. Everyone else seemed to enjoy it too, and it was nice to have Korbin in the general area for once, since he spent most of his time stuffed away in his office.

"Hey, guys!" Eric walked into the room, Katie following behind. "Look at this buffet of deliciousness."

Katie watched Stephanie glance at Eric's ass before winking and straightening her face.

"Morning," Calvin said through a full mouth. "Grab some plates and chow down."

"Ah, no thanks." Katie smiled and poured a cup of java. "I'm good with my coffee."

"Me too." Eric nodded. "But thanks for the offer."

"What's up with you two?" Damian asked, glancing over his paper. "Neither of you ate dinner last night either, and except for garbage disposal Calvin you guys are the biggest eaters in the house."

"Yeeeahh…" Eric grinned. "We kind of have something going on today that will require empty stomachs."

"If it's gross don't say it," Calvin told them, still through a full mouth.

"No, not gross," Katie said. "Exciting, and I'm more than ready for it."

"We have decided to go after the prize in a donut-eating contest the radio station is putting on," Eric informed them excitedly.

"That's cool," Stephanie exclaimed. "I know Katie can put back some freaking donuts, but are you up to it, Eric?"

Eric took a sip of his coffee. "Always."

"Pandora can put back donuts." Katie laughed. "I'm just

the vessel, but today I am not allowing any help. I don't want to cheat."

"Well then, I smell a field trip," Damian replied, grinning at Korbin.

"Hell, yeah," he agreed. "I wouldn't miss this for the world. I'm taking bets on who blows chunks first."

"Come *on*," Calvin whined, pointing at his mouth. "But yeah, I'm in. Damian drives!"

"I'll get the signs ready. Gotta cheer on my girl." Stephanie winked. "And you too, Eric, but let's face it— she's got you by at least three donuts."

"We'll see," he replied, rolling his eyes. "We will *definitely* see."

General Brushwood took a deep breath and leaned back in his chair, staring into space. His mind was in another place; he was getting ready to meet with Jehovivich to talk about her attitude and everything that had recently happened between her and the demons.

He had received her file, and though there was an obvious reason for what was going on, it wasn't as black and white as he had hoped. She was good at her job, no doubt about that, but the issue needed to be addressed.

He was stirred from his thoughts by a knock on his door. "Come in," he called, sitting up in his chair.

"Morning, sir." Jehovivich stepped inside. "You wanted to see me?"

"Yes. Please sit down." He pointed to the chair in front of his desk.

She nodded but paused as she sat, staring at her open file on the desk. She looked up at him and cleared her throat, sitting the rest of the way down and placing her hands in her lap. He pushed the papers around and took a deep breath, putting his fingers to his lips.

"That's my file," she began. "Am I in trouble?"

"No," he replied, "but we should go over some things."

He turned the paper over and leaned forward to read through her service record.

"You have an impeccable record, Colonel. You have received six different awards, seven ribbons, an exemplary rating from every command, and you have never visited sickbay since you entered the service. You don't take vacations, you don't take leave, and you put your nose to the grindstone."

"This is more than a career for me, sir," she told him. "It is my life. I will have plenty of time to take vacations when I am out of the service."

"Right," the general agreed. "You *are* a distinguished soldier."

"Thank you, sir" she replied.

"*BUT*…you have a very black-and-white attitude about killing demons. You have this outlook that all demons are bad, no matter whether they are allies or not. You almost despise the human that has been infected, regardless of the fact that it wasn't their fault. In this line of work that can be a serious problem, and it raises a warning to me on how to handle you around the mercenaries. I *want* to trust you, but part of me fears that I will turn around one day and find that you have shot our ally in the back with one of their own bullets. We need to discuss this, because if we are going to move forward I need to understand where you are coming from."

She looked at him for a moment before answering. "I would never do that unless it was a direct order from you or a superior and they posed a significant threat."

"I want to believe that," the general replied. "And I appreciate your dedication and loyalty to the service, but that *still* does not explain your mindset toward the Damned and demons."

She sat there silently for a moment, trying to find the words. "I don't know what you want me to tell you, sir. I don't know if you want me to change the way I feel or just push it into the background. I have assured you that I am more than aware of my duty and would never sacrifice that because of my personal feelings."

"Your personal feelings *are* getting in the way," he replied, picking up a manila envelope.

He pulled out a stack of papers and flipped through until he found the spot. They were medical records for psych evaluations from before she was in the military.

"The patient, after trauma, refers to the accused as a demon with red eyes and no soul," he read out loud. "The patient has a deep-seated hatred toward the 'demons of the world,' as she puts it. She exhibits no sign of mental instability, but further reviews and therapy will be needed to push past the events experienced."

"Those are confidential."

"*Nothing* is confidential when it comes to the security of the United States," the general countered. "You didn't disclose these evaluations or what they were for to the military when you joined. You know as well as I do that if the wrong person sees these records they could easily discharge you. This could put your entire career in jeopardy, which would be a shame since it has been so distinguished."

"What do you want me to say?" She sighed. "I didn't want it to hurt my chances of getting into the military, and I had already been recruited into the program. I just wanted to put it behind me."

"That would have been fantastic, only it is rearing its ugly little head right now." Brushwood looked at her. "You want to know what you should say? How about we start with the truth, because I need to understand where you are coming from on this or I will have no other recourse but to turn these files over to IA and let them know what I have discovered. Please, give me a reason not to do that."

"Fine." She let out a deep breath and rubbed her face before relaxing in the chair. "Before I came into the military I had a very good friend, someone I had grown up with. She changed one day—like a complete one-eighty—and the only thing I could come up with was that she was demon-possessed. She did terrible things to me; *horrible* things, so I hate them. I hate demons. I hate anything that can seep into a person and change them into a monster like that."

The general nodded as he listened, trying to be understanding of what she had gone through. He wasn't going to turn her in—and probably wasn't even going to replace her —but he did need to know that it was safe to let her out in hostile situations with demon-killing bullets, side by side with the Damned teams. She could easily start a war between the military and the mercs just by giving into that anger in a combat situation. It was a serious risk, but she deserved the right to explain herself.

Brushwood turned the page and ran his finger down it, stopping and looking up at her. "Candice Johnson?"

"Yeah." She nodded sharply. "Candice Johnson."

She shook her head and chuckled softly. The general tilted his head at her reaction. She seemed to accept talking about her pretty well, but whatever this girl had done still affected the colonel to this day.

"It's funny how for the longest time I thought we were friends. Best friends, even." She stared toward the windows, her voice calm for all the anger she must be holding in. "As a child you are so innocent. You are willing to believe and trust those around you. You think you know your friends and their lives and their thoughts, but then they go and surprise you. Those are the moments where that innocence is ripped away and you realize the world is made up of some pretty nasty things."

"The girl's record says that after the events that occurred with you she was put into home care," he told her. "Her symptoms only got worse, though; she was attacking the help, the nurses. Even her parents."

"She had rich parents and they wanted her to be comfortable...and for their *reputation* to stay sterling," Jehovivich answered. "So they called in favors and got her remanded to the house with care. They didn't understand that the demon inside her was growing stronger by the moment." She turned her eyes to him. "She couldn't be caged, you know? She just got angrier and angrier."

"It says here that when she was twenty-four she was seen by a psychiatrist who was connected to us in some way," the general continued. "There is a laundry list of issues including personality disorder, borderline schizophrenia, PTSD, and the list goes on. However, she was given the all-clear on our end."

"What? I mean, that can't be," the colonel exclaimed, reaching for the paper. "I remember the way she could look right through me. How could any person do the things she did to me without having a dark and powerful demon inside her? There had to have been some mistake. She was a *demon*. That was one of the reasons I was so drawn to this program; it gave me a chance to help someone else so they didn't turn into Candice."

"I'm sorry, Colonel," the general said kindly. "The truth is she was simply a sick person. She had no demon in her."

"*I'll be damned,*" Jehovivich mouthed and read through the report.

14

The loud music pulsated through the crowd and the lights shimmered through the smoke-filled arena.

The cheers could be heard for miles as the bands grooved to the melodic tones of their instruments. The scene was wild and on fire—just the way Brock liked his shows.

He was a newly-minted star and had been traveling with his band full time for the last six months. The record company they signed with had made it a sweet deal with a classic band bus, hotel rooms in every city, and only the best treatment.

It was unlike anything Brock or the band had ever experienced, since they had grown up in small-town America.

Brock grabbed the microphone stand and sang hard, giving it all he had. He laughed and grinned as he threw back his long sweaty blond hair and stared into the crowd with his bright blue eyes. In the front row girls swooned and screamed, reaching their arms out for just one chance to touch the golden god on the stage.

The guitar solo went on and on, and Brock bobbed his head up and down as he smiled at a hot redhead in the front row who ceremoniously lifted her top and flashed her big fake tits. He glanced at the bassist, who gave him the universal hand sign for "rock on," and Brock stepped back to the mic, signaling the end to the solo.

The boys finished their set on a high from the attention of the crowd, the lights, and the size of the stage. When the last note of the last song faded there was a moment's pause before the crowd erupted into cheers.

Brock put his hands into the air and leaned toward the mic. "Thank you, everyone," he screamed, waving to the people on the floor, then those in the upper seats. "We love you!"

The guys ran off-stage and out of sight, panting and laughing, the adrenaline still rolling through their blood. The concert staff handed them all towels and water bottles and they moved back into the alley where the artists prepared for their set.

The next band was getting ready to go on and they stared in awe over at the hottest new rock band in America.

"That was fucking *golden*," the guitarist exclaimed, high-fiving Brock. "The way that rhythm moved over the crowd —and the way the chicks jumped up and down. *Fuck* yes."

"It looks as if our night may not quite be over yet." Brock smiled, turning the guitarist toward the gaggle of groupies down the alley who were whispering and giggling as they stared at the band.

"That's what *I'm* talkin' about!" The guitarist tapped the singer's chest. "I get the brunette with the belly ring."

"You can have as many as you like." Brock turned to his bandmates and put his hands in the air. "There are plenty to go around, boys, but first we have to go sign those autographs we promised the company."

"How many chicks do you think you can get back to the bus?" the drummer asked. "You know, since we are jamming out of here tonight? There won't be any crazy hotel parties like in LA."

"Hi, there," a blonde girl purred, strutting past Brock in a short jeans skirt and crop top.

"Well, hello," he replied, watching her as she continued down the alley. "Good *lord* this is going to be an exhausting night."

"Not too exhausting, I hope," the keyboard guy said. "We have three shows in three cities in three days coming up."

"Aw, come on," Brock replied, putting his arm around him as they walked toward the autograph table. "You need to lighten up a bit and relax. Besides, it's not like I have to do that much work. I just lay back and let them take the reins."

"Righht, like last time…when somehow the mattress ended up in the swimming pool at that very expensive hotel." The keyboardist laughed. "One day we are going to find ourselves at the Motel 6."

"Hey, I put that mattress back. It's now a waterbed." Brock chuckled, taking the pen from the venue staff and turning toward the line of fans—mostly girls—waiting to hear from him. "Who's first?"

As Brock went through the line he glanced at the group standing at the edge of the stage. That hot little blonde had joined them and he smiled, unable to turn his head away.

There was just something about her and way she ran her hand down the back of the redhead next to her. He chuckled to himself, thinking that he really loved his fucking life.

There was no way he wasn't getting both of them, and probably more than that.

"They are toying with us," the guitarist said, signing a picture and handing it to the next giggling girl in line. "They are playing hard to get."

"Ha." Brock laughed. "The only thing hard they're gonna get is my—"

"Hi, I'm Jemma," a little girl said, stopping him in his tracks.

"Hi there, Jemma," he replied, signing her poster. "Thanks for coming out. Do you want to take a picture with me?"

The little girl smiled and nodded so Brock bent down next to her and smiled for the camera, glancing at the group of girls to see their reactions. Almost all of them swooned, but the blonde just stood there a sexy smirk on her lips, arms folded across her chest.

She was a feisty one, that was for damn sure.

He thanked the little girl again and went back to signing, feeling the deep stare of the group the whole time. He loved it, and he had already picked out the ones he wanted to take back to the bus. He shook his head, thinking just how much rock-'n-rolling he was gonna do that night.

There was a reason the church didn't like it.

Across the way the gathered girls chatted about their clothes, the music, and basically talked up the band like they had been sent by God. The blonde chuckled as she watched Brock put on a display for them.

She turned back to the group on the stage and smiled at her friend. "I think it's amazing how they think they are in control. What they don't get is that we give them exactly what *they* want, and we take exactly what *we* want."

"True," the redhead replied, looking around. "I have to admit that sometimes the fangirl shit gets a little old, but whatever they need to stroke their egos."

They listened to the other fans. "The drummer is just so hot, I wonder if he will actually want to talk to me," one of the girls said.

"Of course not," the blonde told her. "You're new to the game and that's okay, but remember this—these boys want it hot and they don't want to put in a lot of work for it. Let them go on and on about their endless fame and fortune but remember what you are there for: to get your rocks off with a hot guy. Don't get your feelings hurt when he sends you on your way with a band t-shirt as a parting gift."

"Yeah, and if it's really good, you'll know," the redhead added. "You'll be wearing that t-shirt out of the party and nothing else."

"That's what *I'm* saying." The blonde laughed. "I'm calling dibs on Brock, the lead singer."

There was a collective gasp from the group.

"Don't worry, girls. If you think he is going to pick only

one of us you have another think coming." She smiled. "We'll be best friends by the end of the night, and also share a common memory of steamy bus windows. Just remember, don't be one of those girls leftover in the morning that they send off still half-fucked on drugs. Be classy, and don't get so messed up that you pass out. Of course, I always tell you ladies this, and I'll be passing at least half of you looking like someone else's bad lunch on the way to the gym in the morning."

The girls giggled, thinking about what the next few hours would bring. The next band was rocking out onstage, but these girls had come for Brock and his band. The blonde turned from the girls and looked at Brock, swaying her hips as she ran her hands over her stomach. The redhead joined her, dancing close to the blonde and letting their bodies rub together.

Brock glanced at them and the blonde smirked when he tried desperately not to let his mouth fall open.

He was in shock—and he loved every bit of it—but that wasn't a surprise to the girls. They were there seeking *exactly* what the guys wanted to give them.

Exactly who was the stalker and who was the stalkee?

"Ka-tie! Ka-tie! Ka-tie!" Stephanie chanted, thrusting her sign in the air.

Katie looked up at Stephanie with a smirk, showing her a determined face. The MC was blaring music from some new rock band and Katie actually kind of liked it.

She looked at Eric, whose huge eyes were staring at the

two platters of donuts in front of him. He latched onto his glass of milk with one hand and steadied himself. The others were straight-faced and serious; Katie had a feeling those guys were in it to win it.

"All right, everyone," the announcer called, enjoying the little parade of people-watching. "Welcome to the Third Annual Donut-Eating Contest for Charity!"

The crowd whooped and hollered as he pointed to the table.

"Our contestants look prepared, donuts courtesy of Pinkbox Donuts," he continued, clapping in appreciation. "Everyone here today will receive a free donut from Pinkbox, which you can pick up on your way out. All proceeds from today's events go to the Las Vegas Rescue Mission. Visit online for information, and if you got a little extra time stop by and volunteer. These folks could really use the help."

He handed his papers off to a helper and rolled up his sleeves before turning to the contestants. "All right, contestants, the rules are easy: eat the most donuts in the allotted time and you will receive the grand prize...two dozen free donuts a week for one year from Pinkbox Donuts, and they will also donate *five thousand dollars* to Las Vegas Rescue Mission in your name. Everybody on your mark— at the sound of the horn begin."

The crowd went silent as the announcer held his fingers in the air, counting down from five.

Katie shuffled her butt in the seat and looked at Eric excitedly.

When the horn blew she dove in, grabbing two donuts and stacking them on top of each other. She plowed through them, sprinkles and icing flying everywhere. Eric ate his first one in huge bites, finishing it in just seconds.

"Yeah!" Stephanie yelled, bouncing up and down with her signs that read, Go Kandora!

She thought she was clever, and Korbin just laughed and shook his head. Calvin made his way to the edge of the stage and looked up at Eric who seemed to be slowing down after rolling through six donuts. Eric took a deep breath and sipped his milk, as he reached for another.

"Man, you can do this," Calvin exclaimed, acting like a coach. "Don't let Katie beat you again or I'm personally taking your man card."

"Oh, HELL no!" Eric glanced at Katie, who was halfway through her first platter.

He sped up again, chomping hard into the pastries, but it didn't last long. He huffed and puffed and peeked at Katie, who looked like she might just barf.

They gazed down the line of contestants and realized their competition had finished their first tray already.

"Holy shit!" Katie turned to Eric. "They're like fucking professional donut-eaters."

Pandora giggled. *I could spike you into overdrive.*

No, no cheating, Katie replied.

"I give up," Eric moaned. "There's no way we will even make it into the top three."

"I'm right there with you, bud." Katie leaned back and rubbed her stomach. "These people are my heroes."

Pandora scoffed. *Pfft...amateurs.*

They pushed their platters away and cheered on the others. It was a fun time for all of them; something normal, not demon-related for once.

That was why Katie had wanted to do it on her own. She'd wanted just to be human for a moment.

When the buzzer sounded the judge walked down the line, grabbing the hand of a large man at the end of the table and raising it into the air. They stayed to watch the ceremony, and the donut shop handed everyone who participated a dozen donuts. Both Eric and Katie handed theirs to the others, since they didn't want to even *look* at another donut by that point.

"That was one hell of a try, folks," Korbin said smiling. "You are a lot hell of a lot braver than I am."

"Ugh, no more donuts." Eric rubbed his extended stomach. "Like, *ever*."

"How about we all head over to Torn Asunder?" Damian suggested. "First round is on me."

Stephanie clapped. "Sounds good to me."

"I hope they have tea," Katie replied.

Calvin chuckled. "You are so weird sometimes."

Katie raised an eyebrow. "Only sometimes?"

"Okay, all the time," Calvin admitted. "I was just being nice." He scratched his face. "Not sure it'll stick, personally."

The group headed to the bar, talking and laughing about the contest. Eric had never seen people who could eat like that before, at least not where he'd grown up. Damian had apparently witnessed the phenomenon more than once.

"Seriously?" Damian shrugged. "Try watching a hot dog-eating contest. That's fascinating and disgusting in equal parts."

Katie shook her head. "Oh god, that makes me want to puke."

"I'm assuming there will be no more eating contests of any kind in your future?" Stephanie asked.

"Uh, no, not unless I have the assistance of my demon," Katie replied. "And I'm not sure that is legal in the eating-contest world."

Calvin snorted. "I doubt you'll find it in the rule books."

The group looked over as a fight broke out, but it wasn't anywhere near them. They turned back and everyone smiled, glad to have spent the day together. By the time the waitress had gotten to the table Pandora had taken care of Katie's full stomach, so she ordered nachos. Eric looked at her with wide eyes.

She shrugged. "I've got a fast metabolism."

"Yeah." Calvin scoffed. "There is hyper-speed and then there's…" he jerked a thumb at Katie, "demon-speed."

Katie smirked at Calvin and the rest of them ordered. The drinks flowed, the conversation was fantastic, and not once did anyone bring up work. It was a great time out, which they all desperately needed.

Katie had a feeling in her gut that it would be one of the last fun times for a while.

15

"My favorite part of the whole thing was when that plate of asparagus landed in Calvin's lap," Katie said snickering. "It was like one of those slow-motion moments in movies."

"Yeah, that was hot," Calvin said. "And I don't mean that in a good way. The butter was fucking *hot*."

Everyone exited the elevator and stood outside the doors, still laughing. It was nighttime but not that late, and none of them really wanted to call it an evening yet.

Katie hadn't laughed that much in a very long time, and it was the first time she had seen Damian completely into everything that was going on.

She missed Derek, but it was nice seeing the team start to close ranks and be a family once more. She knew that was part of what made everyone fight harder during battles. It made a huge difference when you had something personal to fight for.

She was convinced that if every team were as close as theirs was, mortality rates would be a lot lower overall.

"Hey, we haven't watched the soap in a bit," Katie exclaimed. "We have like three episodes in the queue. You guys up for it?"

"Hell, yeah," Stephanie agreed.

"What she said," Korbin replied a bit less enthusiastically.

"I have been dying to find out what happened to the captain of the ship that was lost at sea," Eric interjected.

"And that hot number..." Calvin snapped his fingers. "What was her name again?"

"Melissa," Katie told him, then looked at Damian. "What about you, D? You have something else going on?"

"I do," Damian replied, making everybody groan. "But it can wait. I might as well get in on the fun."

"Hell, yeah!" Calvin slapped him on the shoulder. "Sit with me and I'll bring you up to speed."

"I will never admit this to anyone," Damian assured Calvin as they walked toward the main room. "Not in a confessional. Not even on my deathbed."

"You know the saying..." Damian replied. "What happens in Vegas..."

Katie laughed and went into the kitchen to make some bright blue sugar popcorn.

This time she made four bowls, which was enough for everyone to go nuts. Pandora was more than excited about it; she had gotten donuts and soaps in the same day and hadn't even been required to beg or threaten Katie's life.

It was a miracle.

Don't get used to it. Katie smiled. *I am enjoying the day though.*

You know what? Pandora replied. *I am too, but I'll take it to Damian's grave, so don't go using that statement on me in the future.*

Katie carried the bowls into the living room. *You really need to have a little bit more faith in humanity.*

"Great, more sugar." Eric groaned. "I'm gonna be Wilfred Brimley in his diabetes commercials by the end of the night."

Katie patted him on the head and stuck out her lower lip with a "poor baby" face before plopping down in her chair. They started the first one, fast forwarding through the opening scenes. The family and friends of the people lost at sea were in the first scene, then in walks the hero— the guy who had survived just about everything.

"Shh shh shh…" Stephanie leaned forward. "They are going to tell us what happened to the ship."

"I have news about the ship," the character said.

"No shit," Eric replied, rolling his eyes.

"SHHHHHH!" Katie, Stephanie, and Calvin hissed simultaneously.

"We have combed the area repeatedly, but there is no sign of the ship or any wreckage. There weren't even any calls for help. It's almost like it just disappeared. We are obviously continuing the search and will let you know if anything is found."

"I knew it!" Calvin slapped his knee. "That motherfucking ship went for a sail on the River Styx."

"You think?" Stephanie asked. "You think it was swallowed by a portal?"

"Hell, yeah I do," Calvin told her. "It's a ship full of white folks, so you know something crazy happened to that bunch."

"What about Raymond?" Eric pointed out. "He was black and he was on the boat."

Calvin tsked. "Yeah, that brother is dead too. You watch." He shook his head.

The show came back from commercial to a scene in a dark dank cave where the survivors of the missing ship were huddled. There were bodies lined up along the walls and the main female character was standing with her arms crossed.

"How many dead?" one of the characters asked.

"Over two dozen that we've found," she told them. "Still many unaccounted for. But there's something I want you to see."

The main character walked over and lifted a sheet, revealing Raymond's body.

"SEE! I told you motherfuckers! Brother is deader than a doornail," Calvin laughed and shook his head. "I *knew* it was too good to be true."

"Maybe they will resurrect him," Korbin offered.

"Only works through the midway portal," Katie explained. "They look like they are in the hell portal."

"This is the *dumbest* conversation I've ever had," Korbin told them all with a blank face.

"Really?" Katie replied, turning around and looking at him. "With *this* team? I would have thought there would have been much more idiotic conversations."

He looked up at the ceiling a moment before answering, "You may be right."

The crew watched all three episodes without a single argument breaking out, which was a record for them.

They laughed and joked through the whole thing, making the base feel like a home for the first time—at least to Katie. When it was over everyone went their separate ways, figuring it was time for bed.

Katie lingered in the main area for a moment, unable to escape that nagging feeling in her stomach.

I have it too, Pandora shared. *So it's not gas.*

What is it? Katie asked.

Not sure, but whatever is coming may just be bigger than we think.

Brock signed the last of the autographs for the evening and glanced at the groupies. They giggled and looked away and Brock smiled, handing over the last photo and capping his marker. He turned to his guitarist, who was finishing up his autographs as well.

"We are getting closer," he whispered.

"Yeah, but we don't want to come off as *too* desperate," the guitarist replied. "We want to keep them thinking we are badass musicians who don't give two shits."

"We *are* badass musicians who don't give two shits," Brock responded. "Watch and learn, my friend."

Brock tugged his leather vest down and swished his hand through his hair, then cleared his throat and sauntered over to the girls.

They smiled and spread out into a line of sorts, and he walked straight past the redhead and blonde to the least attractive of the group, a brunette. He knew that if he favored the one everyone would turn their nose up at, the girls would work even harder to get him. Besides, for being the least attractive of the group, she was still pretty damn hot.

He walked back down the line and chose the redhead, waving his finger at her and watching her as she swayed over on her six-inch platform heels.

Brock knew the blonde wanted him, and he could see her poise begin to waver as he walked past her again. She thought she was hot shit—like no one could touch her—but he wanted her to know who was in control. After the band had lined up to make their selections, he walked back to the blonde and leaned toward her to put his lips next to her ear.

"You can come too," he whispered.

His three girls surrounded him and he put his arms around two of them and started walking toward the bus.

"They're all yours, boys," he called over his shoulder. "Hell, bring 'em all if you want."

When they climbed into the bus there was already music blaring and booze set out. The girls giggled as they walked through, running their hands over the leather seats.

Brock poured himself a glass of whiskey and took a sip, trying not to show his distaste for straight liquor. He wanted to come off as a badass and he thought that would do the trick.

"Ladies, let's get some privacy from the rest of the party," he suggested, leading them to a door in the back.

It was a bedroom furnished with a huge California king bed and a fully stocked bar. The girls giggled as they entered the room and all three sat down on the edge of the bed.

He closed the door, took off his vest, and sipped his drink.

"Blondie, why don't you pour you and your ladies some champagne?"

She got up, popped the cork of a bottle of bubbly in an ice bucket on top of the bar, and poured three glasses. When she went back to distribute the champagne she noticed a plain brown box with a game sticking out of the top of it on the side table. She handed out the glasses and wandered over to it, pulling Mirror Mirror out.

"You like games?" she asked, turning around and holding it up. "I've heard this one is real; that you can *really* summon demons with it. That was why they recalled it."

"Oh yeah?" He smirked as he put his arm around her waist. "And what do I have to do to summon *your* demon?"

She smiled enthusiastically. "We should play this."

He groaned and pulled the game from her hands, tossing it to the floor.

"Play *later*. Let's fool around now," he told her, pulling her down on the bed with the other two.

They all rolled around on the bed, teasing and playing. Brock laid his head on the brunette's lap as the other two began to undress him. The girl ran her hands through his long blonde hair and started massaging his scalp. He closed his eyes as the women took care of his needs, just relaxing from the long trip and the long night.

"Where are you from?" the brunette asked.

"He's from Wyoming," the redhead told her.

"Yeah, but *where* in Wyoming?"

"I am from Archfiend, Wyoming," Brock answered. "It's small. You won't even find it on a typical map. Maybe a thousand people live there."

"Small-town boy," the blonde teased. "I like that. Hopefully you'll forget your manners tonight."

He turned his head and grinned at her, thinking about his hometown. It had been a long time since he had been there, or at least felt like it. He had come up in the world and made something out of himself; something more than just a farmer or rancher.

He had gotten out, but sometimes he *missed* it.

"What is it like there?" the brunette asked.

"Quaint." Brock smiled. "There are two stoplights and five stop signs in the whole place, and really the only reason they were put there was to figure out who was at fault if there was a wreck. I'm pretty sure I was personally responsible for at least two of those stop signs, I didn't really give a shit about the speed limit."

He groaned and sat up, then looked at the three beautiful women. He still couldn't believe that *he* was the guy with the groupies. His mother had always told him he was too smart for the rock-and-roll lifestyle and that he should be something bigger.

But he had wanted it so badly, and by using his smarts he had finally had gotten here.

He planned on enjoying every little second of it, too.

"Now, enough about me," he told them, eyes darkening with mischief. "Let's talk about you...and you...and *definitely* you."

As he pointed to each girl he ran his finger down her chest. They giggled and started to undress.

He sat back on the bed and put his arms behind his head, just watching the action. He was going home in a month when they got a break from touring, but until then he was going to enjoy this life.

All of his friends and most of his family, even if they wouldn't admit it, were jealous as hell of the lifestyle of the rock and roll guys they had become. He had felt the same way about the rockers he had listened to growing up, and now he was one.

Brock had always been hugely into girls and he was a charmer, the guy who could get almost any woman to fall for him.

He knew how to read people, and that helped him maneuver his way through not only women but life as well. He was the lead singer of the band, and his charm and charisma impressed most people he came into contact with.

He paused a moment in his reflection to admire their bottoms. Nice!

Even before the label had signed them and helped them produce better music they'd had a following, mostly due to Brock and his alluring personality, big charming grin, and mischievous eyes.

And while he might have power over women, they also had power over him. He had been known to fall for a gorgeous smile and a pair of perfect breasts in a heartbeat.

His drummer teased him, saying his mission was to fall in love in every city in America.

Brock sighed. It wasn't love. It was lust.

He loved himself, and his career and he would never

trade that for some chick, even though many tried their best to get in there with him.

No, he was more than happy letting his fine groupies fight it out for a night in the back of his bus. Going home was gonna be a much-needed rest for him and his dick for *damned* sure.

As the girls closed in on him, he turned his head and briefly stared at the box on the floor. He winced slightly as a flash of heat blew through his head, but he figured it was the whiskey and ignored it. It was just a stupid game, right?

He turned his attention back to the women and drowned himself in pleasure for the rest of the night.

16

"I don't get this part of it." Travis sighed and looked at Joshua.

"That's not important; not to you, anyway. It is part of my process." Joshua closed his books. "You can do your jobs without that information."

"Right," Travis replied, watching him walk away.

He still wasn't sure how what he was doing changed the raw material into the special metal that came out the other side.

He had been told what the metal did, but that meant there had to either be a specific metal that demons reacted to...or it was magic.

Seeing as Travis didn't believe in magic, he had to be missing something. It was either a material not in the recipe or it was the sequence in which the product went together.

Travis, incredibly frustrated, went over to his computer and opened the private server. He put the new information in, then glanced around the room to make sure that no one was watching him and pulled up the last email from his boss. He grimaced; the man was pissed.

He didn't understand why it was taking Travis so long to figure everything out. He didn't understand what the weapons actually did, so he didn't understand that there was a piece Travis couldn't figure out.

Nonetheless, he had been ordered to send the information he'd gathered so he opened his notes and typed a quick message. He didn't like this assignment. He had to go behind people's backs, which wasn't what he had signed up for.

This was supposed to be an easy operation, but he actually liked Joshua and the women who worked there.

Still, he had worked his ass off to get a high position with that company and he wasn't going to fuck it up because he had a moral crisis. He finished the email and looked it over really fast, shaking his head. He opened the encryption app but as he started the process the door opened and Korbin walked in. He hit the escape button and sent the email in haste before closing his laptop and notes and walking away from the area.

"Hey, Stephie-poo," Calvin said, stopping in the door of the IT room. "Haven't seen this up and running since Derek was alive."

"Yeah, I figured I would get some of the stuff moving. Don't want to waste the money we sank into this thing."

"I don't understand all this stuff," Calvin told her, looking at the different screens.

"Well, this is the security system—which *should* have stayed up, but someone overlooked that." Stephanie pointed at a bank of screens showing different angles of the base. "The rest of this stuff is surveillance and ops... trying to get information before someone else does."

"Right." Calvin walked along the bank of computers, stopping at the last one and tilting his head. "And what does this one do?"

"That one?" Stephanie looked over her shoulder. "Oh, that's just a monitor of outgoing communications from anyone in the base. It's a good protective measure in case we ever have a rogue teammate or something."

"Is it supposed to be flashing red?"

Stephanie stopped and turned slowly, walking over to the screen. She looked at the text line, which told her it was an email sent from Joshua's building. She pulled up the outgoing message.

"Uh-oh. Looks like one of our government boys is breaking the rules. I should probably go take care of him."

Calvin grabbed her arm. "Wait, you should probably go to Korbin on this. It's a sensitive one."

"You're right." She sighed. "Thanks."

Stephanie jogged through the tunnels to Korbin's office. He was just coming back and glanced curiously at her as she followed him in.

"You look like you are on a mission," he offered, one eyebrow raised. "What's up?"

"This." Stephanie handed Korbin a printout of the email. "Sent ten minutes ago from Joshua's building."

Korbin read it and sighed as he sat down in his chair. "I'd better call Katie in."

When Katie arrived they told her about the situation. She was fuming mad, but Korbin was able to calm her enough to keep her from heading over there and ripping his head from his shoulders.

Korbin called the general on speakerphone and Katie gave him the details.

"So that," she finished, "is where we are."

"Hold tight," Brushwood requested. "I'll be there in four hours. Don't let him know there's anything going on. We'll take care of this immediately."

After they hung up they all looked at each other for a minute, trying to figure out what the next steps should be. Katie raised her hands to her head and began to pace. Korbin shook his head and looked at Stephanie.

"Thanks for catching this," he told her. "It's important to keep that IT room up and running even if we don't know how to use everything." He tapped a finger on the desk. "*I* have no idea how to use it."

"Noted," Stephanie answered. "Calvin is over there right now keeping an eye on things."

"Thanks." Korbin turned. "Katie, I need you to calm down and then go over to the building and keep an eye on Travis. We don't want him to run. That would not be good for him. Act like nothing is wrong, and as soon as the general gets here we will meet you over there."

"All right," Katie said through clenched teeth. "But he owes you his thanks for restraining me, because I want to rip his fucking face off."

Korbin and Stephanie followed Katie through the

tunnels to the elevator and Katie headed to Joshua's building while Stephanie and Korbin went to the helo pad to wait for the general, even though he would be a while yet.

They sat there for hours, just enjoying a little peace and quiet before everything hit the fan.

It was a good thing. Korbin needed to calm down, and Stephanie wanted that time with him. When the helicopter got there it was just Brushwood and Jehovivich. He nodded at Korbin and the two of them headed for the building.

The general pulled out his cell and called Travis's boss. "There has been a breach of security by *your* man. I don't want to hear your excuses at this point. I will be putting you in listen-only mode when we walk into the building. I want you to understand how grave this issue really is."

The general pushed into the building and marched toward Travis. Jehovivich went behind him and cuffed him, then stepped to the side.

"What the hell?" Travis looked from person to person, his eyes large. Korbin walked over to Travis and gripped his arm tightly.

"You are to stop all research immediately. You sent highly-classified information through the internet to your boss," the general told him. "We were unable to download the attachment. We can only imagine it contained even more information than you stated in the body of the email."

Stephanie held the printed copy of the email up in front of Travis's face and his eyes fell in shame. She grimaced in disgust, sick and tired of everyone trying to hurt them, and walked back to where Katie was standing, arms crossed and eyes flaring red.

"Do you remember what I said about security here?" Brushwood asked. "I told you if you fucked with this you would find yourself in an unmarked grave."

"General, I—"

The general raised his pistol and pulled the trigger.

The room was silent as he unmuted the video feed. Travis's boss was freaking out. His hands shaking and he was barely able to say a word. The general straightened his jacket and took a deep breath.

"We will be talking shortly," he informed the man. "I expect you to return every shred of data he sent you... unless, of course, you want to share his grave."

"This is completely unacceptable," the CEO yelled completely beside himself. "You *murdered* that man. You will *not* get away with this!"

"We are at war, asshole," the general shouted. "There are no rules. He was a traitor and a danger to the people on this base. I promise you I will do the same to you if you decide to become a traitor as well."

"Fine, fine." The CEO shrugged. "I had him send me the information. I thought if we could replicate the process we could offer the same tools cheaper. There was no harm meant."

"You're fucking *fired*," the general snarled. "And you will send that data *now*."

The general terminated the call, handed the cell to Jehovivich, and looked at Korbin, who was shaking his hand out and wincing. The metallurgist lay unconscious on the ground.

The general had fired the bullet into the wall as Korbin knocked Travis out.

"That kid has a fucking hard jaw." Korbin kept shaking his hand.

"Wake him up," the general directed Jehovivich.

She nodded and bent down, opening a capsule of smelling salts and waving it under his nose. Travis's eyes shot open and he groaned, Korbin and the general grabbed him under the arms and lifted him into a chair.

Brushwood waited for his head to clear. "Welcome to your new life."

"What?" Travis squeaked, looking around. "What do you mean?"

"You are dead now, or at least everyone thinks you are," he told the man as he paced around him. "Now you are part of this mercenary team. My advice is to make the best of your new life, since it's not a crime to shoot a dead man...and don't think I won't."

"And when you can stand properly," Korbin added, pointing behind the man, "you can fix the fucking bullet hole in my wall."

He slowly looked over his shoulder at the hole. He thought he had dreamt the general firing at him, but apparently he hadn't.

Travis had gotten himself into some seriously deep shit, and he wasn't sure what to say.

The general and Korbin walked toward the door, leaving Stephanie, Katie, and now Calvin to look after Travis. Korbin would have thought the whole thing almost comical if their information weren't floating out there somewhere for the demons to find.

They made their way to Korbin's office, where he fixed everyone some coffee.

They sat silently contemplating what had happened for a few minutes. Korbin couldn't believe that the general had done that, but in a way, it had increased his faith in the alliance they were building.

"I'm sorry you had to come all the way out here," Korbin started.

"No, it's all right." Brushwood waved a hand. "This was our fault. He was our contractor, and I'm sorry we put you and your team in harm's way. I should have gone with my gut from the beginning. You never can fully trust contractors. They are in it for the money, not for their country, or the bastards would be serving—though some of them have. Still, no excuse. We will not allow this to happen again, not on our watch."

"Does it really mean that the guy is a mercenary now?" Jehovivich asked.

"Not necessarily," Korbin replied. "He isn't Damned, which makes it more of a prison sentence—not that he doesn't deserve one. But we could wipe part or all of his memory."

"We should probably consider doing that," the general said. "We could wipe this whole ordeal from his memory and let him continue with his job; just lock him out of all communications. He wouldn't be able to get to his boss, and at this point his boss thinks he is dead anyway."

"I agree." Korbin sat back in his chair. "May I ask you something, General?"

"Of course," he replied, chewing on the end of his cigar.

"Would you really have killed him?"

The general smiled and leaned forward with his elbows on his knees. "Son, we are at war. Though not everyone sees the enemy, this is the most important war humanity has ever fought. I do *not* have time to go around teaching adults the meaning of the word 'responsibility.'"

"I'm such a fucking idiot." Travis put his head in his hands.

Calvin nodded at Stephanie and Katie to let them know they could take off. The kid was stupid. Reckless, even, but Calvin almost felt for him.

He didn't realize the seriousness of what he had done. He had just been following orders...only he followed the wrong ones.

He had to pay the price for that since ignorance isn't a defense, but Calvin couldn't help but want to calm his nerves a bit.

"I *knew* I should have listened to the general." Travis shook his head. "But my boss was threatening my job, my future...everything. God, I am such a moron."

"Listen," Calvin began, squatting in front of him, "you need to pull yourself together right now. What's done is done. You should just be thankful you're still alive. We don't have time for pity parties."

Travis just continued to shake his head.

"Hey," Calvin growled, which got his attention. "You know Katie?"

"Yeah?"

"Yeah, well, she was sacrificed to a demon and her life changed in a matter of minutes." Calvin snapped his fingers. "Why? Because she was trying to help some asshole with his chemistry homework. You? You *chose* to make a dick move, so buck the hell up or we can make this permanent."

"Are you saying I can eventually get out of here?"

Calvin thought about how he wanted to answer. "Figure this out and yeah, there *is* a way, but it won't be easy."

"Whatever it is, I'll do it," Travis ground out, standing up. "I'll make this right. I gotta go apologize to Joshua."

Calvin stood up and nodded and Travis grabbed his book and headed to Joshua's desk. He apologized before opening it and detailing everything he had figured out or guessed and what he was still wondering.

The guy had fucked up for damn sure, but Calvin knew that with a little motivation things could get back to normal.

At least he hoped they would.

17

There was a full team meeting that morning; something they hadn't done in a while.

Katie liked the idea.

Everyone had their own job and responsibilities, but on the whole, rank didn't mean much anymore.

Well, Korbin was the leader; there was no question there. But the rest of them worked as a team, the most qualified leading and the rest using their initiative. If they didn't include everyone information might get lost in translation. Besides, they needed all the help they could get now, especially with this rogue hell-demon squad attacking both the military and the mercenaries.

"Thank you for coming, everyone." Korbin stood up. "We are in a precarious position at the moment—we need help, but resources are limited. Any support we acquire right now is going directly to Amy's Assassins, and rightfully so. Her team is down a number of people and they need to get back up to strength."

"While I understand their plight," Eric interjected, "how are the rest of us supposed to do our jobs plus pick up the slack, especially when everyone is hurting?"

"That was exactly what I asked," Korbin replied. "Which is why both the Georgia team and the New York team are sending us redshirts."

"Excellent," Stephanie said. "Any of them into technology?"

"No, but San Francisco is sending a redshirt, an IT guy who was, and I quote, 'playing the *damned* game.'"

Katie snorted. "What in the world does that mean?"

"It means he has a really low-level inexperienced non-aggressive demon," Korbin explained. "But I was told that the guy is whip-smart at hacking and stuff."

"Well, that sounds better than Calvin and me doodling away in there," Stephanie declared.

"I second that." Calvin raised a hand, waving it like he was in a classroom. "Praise Bill!"

"All right!" Korbin clapped his hands. "We also have some feedback from our consultant James Caplan. The intel suggests that attacks in this country are lessening in number, but the severity of the attacks has increased exponentially."

"Oh, that sounds lovely." Eric groaned. "I won't put my life on the line nearly as often, but when I do it will be balls to the wall."

"There is an Accept song for that," Damian remarked. When silence ensued he looked around. "What? Rebellious times call for rebellious songs."

"Eric is right." Korbin moved some paper around on the table. "We have seen an increase in intensity over the course of demon-hunting history, though this is the largest increase at one time."

"I have a question." Katie looked around. "Has anyone ever taken the fight into the demon realm?"

Korbin shrugged. "Not that I'm aware. Anyone else?"

"Does Pandora know?" Damian asked.

"Hold one second, please." Katie looked down at the table.

We have had fights of course, but in general the demons are stronger and tend to swarm anyone who comes into our domain, Pandora replied. *Then you have the Seventy-Two, who attack anything that doesn't belong down there. Usually it's those from the third rung who attack first, mostly because they want to move up. Those in the second and first rungs allow the third to bleed off the major strength before they get involved.*

Sounds like the military, Katie replied.

If someone from a rung above attacks they most likely will be retrieved by Lucifer, unless of course they embarrassed our race with their pitiful efforts," Pandora continued. *"If that happens Lucifer will allow them to stay in the pits for a very long time— I'm talking decades or even a century—as an object lesson.*

So we would have to execute a surgical strike against the upper levels, if possible, Katie stated.

It's possible, but I'm not at all sure what we would accomplish by doing that, Pandora replied.

Katie drummed her fingers on the table as she thought about what Pandora had told her. It sounded complicated and was nothing they were prepared to handle. She finally looked up, realizing that everyone was waiting for an answer.

"Sorry, guys," she said. "I think Pandora and I will have to discuss it further before we even start to talk about it. Apparently it would be much more complicated than I anticipated."

The team meeting went on for another couple of hours, discussing everything from training to off-time activities. Korbin didn't lay down any restrictions, but he wanted everyone to know that they needed to be careful. If they were being hunted they couldn't take unnecessary chances.

Everyone understood that and none of them wanted to be caught with their pants down, literally or figuratively.

"So that just about wraps it up," Korbin finished. "Anybody have questions?"

Calvin raised a hand, then pointed to Eric. "Can we do another donut-eating contest? Eric shoving donuts in his mouth is hilarious."

"No, thanks," Eric replied. "It'll be a long time before I eat another donut."

"Just you wait." Katie stood up, grabbing her tablet. "They're addictive."

"Calvin and Katie, could you two stay behind?" Korbin asked. "I will see the rest of you at training in the morning."

Katie sat back down, smiling at Stephanie as she ran her hand over Katie's shoulder. She really hoped that she wasn't in trouble, since she couldn't remember doing anything stupid in the last few days.

She looked at Calvin, who didn't seem to know what was up either. Once everyone was out of the room Korbin turned to them.

"I need you guys to go fetch the new IT guy," Korbin told them. "You will take the helicopter to McCarran and then take the jet to San Francisco."

"Why are we picking him up?" Katie asked.

"Well, he's a bit skittish and he *is* possessed, so we don't trust him right now," Korbin replied.

"Are you flying us to the airport?" Calvin asked.

"No," Korbin replied, closing his folder. "The helicopter pilot is waiting for you. Just be gentle with our new guy. He is…uh….*special* and his demon has really messed with his head."

Katie raised her eyebrows, but Korbin didn't offer anything else.

Calvin stood up and motioned for Katie to go.

"Shoo!"

They walked out to the waiting helicopter and in a short time they had reached McCarran. Once they were on the plane Katie relaxed a bit. It wasn't a long flight, but it was long enough for her to take a deep breath for the first time that day.

She glanced at Calvin and smiled.

"Doesn't someone have a birthday today?" she asked.

Calvin grinned and looked at her. "I do, but if you get someone to sing *Happy Birthday* to me at some restaurant I'll return the favor six times this year. I'll make sure we're at a Mexican restaurant, too, so you have to wear the sombrero."

"God." Katie grimaced. "That sounds terrible. Here, I'll pinky-promise you."

She stuck out her pinky and linked it with his.

Calvin squinted at Katie. "Don't think I won't cut off that pinky of yours."

What in the hell are you two talking about? Pandora asked.

If you go to a restaurant and if you tell them it's your birthday, they will make the staff sing to you and give you free cake or ice cream or whatever.

Pandora gasped. *That is fucking amazing! We should do it, for the free sweets if for nothing else. Besides, no one has ever sung* Happy Birthday *to me.*

Never? Katie was shocked. *Sounds like you had a terrible childhood.*

We're demons, so we don't really have childhoods, Pandora pointed out.

Still, that's a staple in this country...and this world, actually, Katie told her. *How old are you, anyway?*

Twenty-two. Every year I turn twenty-two—it's really simple that way. Everyone remembers my twenty-second birthday for eternity.

Yeah, right. Katie laughed. *I'm serious, how old? You can tell me. I'm too terrified of getting a hernia or liver disease to out you.*

Let's just say I am the oldest living female, Pandora replied. *We'll leave it at that.*

Timothy Califore stared out the window of the Special Facilities building, watching the people drive over the Bay Bridge in the far-off distance. He sighed, then stepped away from the glass and looked around the room.

There was a two-way mirror on the wall, but he knew

no one was watching him except for whoever was watching the camera monitors. He had already hacked into those and they showed him sleeping on the table. He stared at his reflection in the mirror. His tall pale body was looking quite emaciated those days.

"If only my mother could see me now," he grumbled, rubbing his hands together nervously. "Good thing I'm not dating now. No man would find me attractive."

His demon chuckled. *"I could make the ladies love you."*

I'm gay! How many times do I have to tell you that? he growled. *You may be a thirsty incubus, but that doesn't mean I am going to sleep with women. God, just the thought of it freaks me the fuck out. You need to realize that we are not going to get laid for a very long time.*

So, eventually? the demon said snidely.

Yeah, like when I've gotten you the hell out of me, he snarled.

Timothy looked down at his laptop and sighed. As soon as they had told him two mercenaries would be picking him up he had gone into panic mode.

He didn't like people, nor did he want to be pushed into some mercenary situation.

God forbid he should have to fight anyone. He just might fake passing out to avoid being skewered by some bloodthirsty demon. Heaven forfend he be possessed by a demon who could actually help protect him.

He felt like he was in hell, trapped by one mercenary group and auctioned off to another, and now—worse than anything else—he was having disgusting thoughts about sleeping with women.

It was fucking awful.

He took a deep breath to clear his head. He was in the middle of hacking the security system. He had no idea why they would allow him to keep his laptop when there was internet access, but hey…he wasn't going to complain.

He was just going to quietly make a break for it and hide somewhere far from women. With that thought, the computer beeped and the latch on the security doors unlocked.

"Yes," he hissed, unplugging his laptop and shoving it into his bag. "Next stop, the middle of nowhere."

He laughed stepped into the hall, but before he made it two steps he froze. A tall black man leaned against the wall with his arms across his chest and his feet crossed at the ankle. Next to him was a woman dressed in entirely black spandex who looked about college age. Both had red rings in their eyes, and they looked like they were waiting for something.

"Going somewhere?" Calvin asked.

Holy shit, who is that fine-ass woman? his demon purred. *I need you to jump right on that and hump her leg. Like right now.*

That's fucking disgusting, he whined. *C'mon, help me here a little.*

His demon sniffed the air in Katie's direction and suddenly got very quiet. Timothy could tell he was nervous.

What? What is it?

Oh, hell no, the incubus growled. *That bitch's demon is pure evil. I'm out of here. I'll be hiding until you get away from those freaks. Good luck, buddy, cause you are on your gay-self own. I'm not homophobic, I'm her-phobic. Shit, I might go for dick if she is the other option.*

Wait, where are you going? Don't leave me alone with these two!

Radio silence. Katie and Calvin had stood there watching him twitch; he was obviously either talking to himself or to his demon. Katie looked at Calvin, who returned the gaze and shrugged.

They stepped forward and grabbed him under the arms.

"Hey, what are you doing? You have to check me out."

"We've already done your paperwork," Calvin told him. "We were just seeing if you could hack security."

"Oh, great." Timothy griped. "You *conned* me. I don't know if you know this, but I'm not a fighter. I won't last two seconds in the field. Granted, I am possessed, but he is just a bitch who does nothing but torture me with girls and grossness."

"Great." Katie groaned. "We have a nervous talker on our hands."

They took Timothy straight out of the building and went directly to their plane.

When they got inside Calvin looked at Timothy, who was still rambling wildly, and back at Katie. He put up a finger and shook his head.

"I'm, um… I'm gonna go talk to the pilot." Calvin opened the cockpit door.

"Pussy!" Katie growled. "Leave me alone with Timothy Talksalot. Great. Come on, jabber jaws, let's get you into your seat."

"I could have dealt with a demon possession if it was the least bit intelligent, but instead I get stuck with this Incubus," he remarked as Katie sat him in his seat. "Now I have this disgusting urge to pork a female, and let me tell you...I have *never* wanted to have sex with a woman, not in my entire life. I'm freaking gay, for God's sake."

Oh, this is priceless! Pandora cackled. *A gay guy with an incubus. Seriously, this couldn't get any more hilarious if it tried. Not only that, this creepy hacker-dude looks like Dracula. Kajesus, get some damn sun.*

"Kajesus?"

I'm working on cutting out blasphemy, Pandora replied. *One effort per decade, so get over it.*

All right, I will. Cut him some slack. That has to be tough on the guy. Katie stifled a laugh.

Pandora scoffed. *Oh, relax. His incubus is weak as shit and probably won't even strain him that much once he gets used to it.*

"My demon says your demon is a bitch," Katie blurted. "She says once you get used to him you can pretty much make him *your* bitch."

"Really?" Timothy exclaimed, calming a bit. "That would be *more* than fantastic. I've always wanted a pet."

"Okay, Timmy." Calvin pushed him into the server room. "Here is your play area. Have fun."

Timothy rubbed his chin and gazed around for a moment, then ran his fingers across some of the screens. He looked at Katie, Calvin, and Korbin with a raised eyebrow.

"What?" Katie asked.

"Uh, excuse me but I *hack*, not install servers," he told them. "I mean, I can whistle the tune, sweetie, but we need to get someone who slings metal in here. Who did all this to begin with? Sheesh!"

"Hey, watch it!" Katie stepped forward, but Calvin put his hand in front of her.

"Calm down." Calvin sighed. "Our IT guy, who was a *very* good friend, was recently killed."

"Oh." Timothy put a hand on the back of his head, ruffling his hair as he looked around anywhere but at Katie. "Sorry. But yeah...we need to fix all this for me to work my magic.

No fret—I know some people who would do it for a case of Pabst Blue Ribbon and a wink from Big Tits over there."

He waved his hand at Katie and she narrowed her eyes, opening her mouth but shutting it again as Korbin stepped in front of her. He wrinkled his nose and looked at Calvin, who just shrugged. Korbin sighed and stepped toward Timothy, who immediately shrank down.

"You mean PBR as in the beer?"

"Yeah, that would be the one."

"What kind of person would work for PBR? I mean, it's like the trailer park of beers." Korbin grimaced. "They could at least go for some—shit I don't know—Sam Adams or Heineken, which are still shitty but not piss-water."

"Hey, not all of us are snobbish high-and-mighties okay?" Timothy snapped, turning his back on Korbin and looking at the security screens.

"Whatever." Korbin rolled his eyes. "That won't work anyway, since you can't connect with anyone who knew you before. Those are the rules when we become Damned. You are pretty much dead to everyone in the world except for us. It sucks, I know, but that's how it is. It protects them too. We wouldn't want them getting hurt on our behalf."

"These people don't know me." He scoffed. "Hello, I'm a hacker! We don't have friends. You know that whole public image of hackers sitting in their mom's basement with three computers, a dozen bags of Doritos, and three cases of Mountain Dew? We're usually hacking something on one screen and kicking ass in Halo on the other? Yeah, that's pretty much spot-on for me." He sighed. "I am the walking version of everyone's expectation."

"I thought you said you knew these people?" Korbin asked, crossing his arms over his chest.

"I know their *handles*. That's what we hackers use," he replied. "They have never met me, nor do they know my real name. It's all very black-ops, and luckily I'm a good hacker so there is nothing out there that can trace me back to my real name."

"Well, luckily for you I figured you might need someone to do some extra work to get you off the ground," Korbin told him, pulling out a file. "I have contacts for that. I want to hire someone from Las Vegas. It's too risky to pull people from all over the country. The more noise we make the more likely it is those demon teams will come barreling down here, taking you and your incubus with them."

"That sounds a bit terrifying," Timothy whimpered with wide eyes.

"Don't worry, you are in charge of the security cameras." Korbin smiled. "You'll have a heads-up."

"I need recommendations from your contacts then." He sighed. "And seriously, they better not be shit."

"Already on top of that, boss." Korbin slapped the file down next to him.

"Well, aren't you Mister On Top of Things." Timothy snickered and flipped open the file.

He skimmed through the pages, nodding, groaning, and making every other noise he could emit. Korbin lifted an eyebrow and Katie rolled her eyes and crossed her arms. This guy was not only a pain in the ass but more of a diva than they had first assumed.

"Oh, great." Timothy flipped to the last page. "Just my fucking luck—all females."

"And what's wrong with that?" Katie asked angrily. "You think girls can't match your superior intellect?"

"No," he answered. "I have no problem at all with women setting up the servers, but I would have liked to get some eye candy in here. But nooo...I get the best Vegas has to offer: two bimbos with big boobs and bigger IQs. Seriously, I think you demon people are trying to make this hell on Earth. All I have is the old guy..."

Timothy motioned toward Korbin.

"And Big Scary Guy." He nodded at Calvin.

"I'm not scary," Calvin mumbled. He looked at Katie, who just shrugged.

"I'm sorry we aren't running a dating service." Korbin sighed and grabbed the file. "These people are the best we have to work with under the circumstances."

"I'll go get them," Calvin volunteered, taking the file from Korbin. "I'll have them finish up the server installs in the SUV so we don't get blown up. Load up the SUV and I'll be on my way. The sooner we get this shit done, the safer we will be."

"Mmmhmm," Katie eyed Calvin.

"What?" he asked.

"You just want to see what they look like," she accused him. "You are picturing huge-boobed Vegas dancers. Watch...they'll be goth chicks hissing at the daylight and scared to get near you."

"I'm sorry." Calvin smirked. "When did you mistake me for being gay?"

Katie shook her head and stepped to the side as the guys started carrying the equipment to the van.

———

After Calvin was gone Katie went out into the sunlight.

She closed her eyes for a moment, taking in the warmth and enjoying the breeze blowing across her skin.

There was suddenly beeping in the background, which sounded like a truck backing up. She opened her eyes and squinted toward Joshua's building, where there was a huge truck with its own forklift dropping off enormous amounts of metal. She tilted her head to the side and headed to where Joshua and Travis were watching.

"Hey, guys! What's going on?"

"Metal drop," Joshua explained.

"I see that, but that's quite a bit more than we usually get. Any reason?" Katie asked.

Travis turned to Joshua. "What do you think the best tack will be to figure out the right resonance?"

"That's a good question." Joshua thought for a moment. "At the proper frequency, the dielectric permittivity changes sign from negative to positive and the real part of the dielectric function drops to zero. We can use the formula I showed you."

"Hmmm…" Travis rubbed his chin. "But we have to do it on a mass scale or we will be here for the rest of our lives."

"Of course," Joshua agreed.

"We definitely should separate the metals first," Travis said. "That will make the calculations much easier."

Katie stared back and forth between the two of them, trying not to show that she was completely and totally lost.

She had never realized until that moment just how smart Joshua was—or Travis for that matter, though it seemed more reasonable for him. She had no idea what they were talking about. They might as well have been speaking another language.

Katie had always thought of herself as reasonably intelligent. She'd had a 4.2 on graduating from high school and was on the honors list in college, but apparently she'd missed the class on metal resonance frequencies.

"I'm sorry, Katie," Joshua turned to her. "Did you ask me something?"

"Yeah, but it's okay. I probably wouldn't understand the answer." She chuckled.

Katie had originally come out of the garage to come check on Joshua and Travis, but from the looks of it, they had everything under control.

They were getting their geek on while Katie tried to find out why the front of his building was starting to look like a scrap yard.

I think they had hard-ons, Pandora suggested.

Probably.

She figured Joshua had his reasons, and he *did* have full reign over acquiring what he needed to get the job done. They were basically creating a factory, which would naturally lead to needing more supplies.

She went into the shop and looked around at all the machines.

The place looked totally different than before the contractors had come and she kind of missed the homey feeling she'd gotten before. It was all for the best, though, and the clanging of metal in the back by Charles just added to the effect.

She wandered back to where he was and stared at the table.

"Hey." He smiled. "Glad you stopped by. This is actually perfect timing. We have almost forty boxes of one hundred rounds each, so about four thousand rounds done already."

Katie was a bit shocked. "Wow! I wasn't sure if you guys had even started making them yet."

"Oh, yeah." Charles picked up a bullet. "As soon as we can get the metal figured out I'll be able to get us up to around twenty-five thousand rounds per day easy."

"That's a lot of bullets," Stephanie exclaimed from behind them.

"That's nothing compared to some of the factories I've seen. Their production is insane," Charles told them.

"Let me ask you this," Stephanie began, tilting her head. "With that kind of production you will undoubtedly need help. What kind of manpower—or womanpower—will you need?"

"Honestly?" He rubbed the back of his head. "I'll probably need seven people minimum to run the machines and quality-check the rounds as they come off the manufacturing floor, and that's just looking at a normal five-day work week. If you count the extra two days I'll need a couple more. Of course, I won't be here forever, so I don't really want to include myself in that number."

"Okay." Stephanie bit the inside of her cheek. "If you could excuse Katie and me for a moment, I need to discuss some business stuff with her."

"Of course." He smiled as the two walked to the other side of the room.

"That's a lot of people," Stephanie whispered to Katie. "We have the girls, but they already have important jobs. There's no one else I can bring on who would be trustworthy enough in this kind of environment. There are far too many secrets floating around this place. You are going to need to call the general and ask him for some people."

"I don't know if he will be able to do any better than you," Katie replied, shaking her head. "We can't just let anyone onto the base. That would pose a serious security issue, and we don't have enough people to run a security detail."

"Well, we don't have enough people to put them on bullet duty either. That would be the whole team," Stephanie countered. "The general wants this operation, so he is going to have to do some serious digging and find reliable and safe people for us."

"I'll see what I can do."

"Hey, boss," Katie leaned against the doorway to Korbin's office.

"Hey." He leaned back in his chair. "Come on in."

"Did you see the mighty load of metal they dropped in front of Joshua's building?"

"I didn't, but Stephanie told me about it. I hope they don't leave it there too long."

"Well, from the sound of things—like them possibly

producing upward of twenty-five-thousand rounds a day—they will roll right through that," Katie replied.

"That's damned amazing!" Korbin exclaimed. "That's intense but good. *Really* good. I have a feeling we and the rest of the country are going to need them."

"Agreed. There's just one thing… In order to produce those numbers, Charles is going to need help. I wanted to find out if it was okay if I asked the general for people. Seven, to be exact, who can come here and help with manufacturing."

"Of course. Bring in whatever you need, but make sure the general vets every single one of them," Korbin agreed. "We need to have someone at the gate checking IDs and demon status."

"My only question is where we're going to house all of them?" Katie asked. "There are plenty of places in the tunnels, but I don't think that is a good idea. I suppose I could clean up some of the barracks and put them there for the time being."

"No, no," Korbin replied. "They won't be staying here. They will come in the morning, work, and leave just like any other nine-to-five job. We will run it like a normal business. If we decide to run weekends, we will let Charles handle the scheduling. They will be military, so there aren't any legal limits on the number of hours per week they can work. Just don't *over*work them."

Katie slapped her forehead with the back of her hand and rolled her eyes. How could she have been so dense as to not figure out that solution sooner?

She had been Damned so long now she thought everyone lived like them.

The truth was, they were the minority. They lived even tighter than the military in most situations. They were always on duty, always nearby, and had to stay together. There was no off-base housing, leave, or anything else normal.

"I'll give the general a call," she told him and stood up. "Thanks."

"No problem," he said absently, already making notes about something else.

Katie saw herself out of the office and headed down the tunnel, slowing down and smiling when Calvin approached, followed by two women. Neither was more than okay in the looks department, and she giggled at Calvin's disappointment.

He was disappointed to not get the Vegas dancers, Timothy was disappointed at not getting hot men, and the incubus was going to be disappointed too.

It was one of those moments where Katie was just really enjoying everyone's misery. Served them right for objectifying those poor women.

19

K atie made her way to the kitchen, where she fixed herself some lunch. She sat down at the table to enjoy it.

She figured the general would be back from his lunch right about now so she ate quickly, knowing the situation had to be cemented soon. They were making such good progress with the company she could hardly keep up.

When she was done with her lunch, she headed over to the call room and closed the door. The regular feed had been routed to Korbin since Stephanie was busy at the shop, and the room had a landline. Her cellphone was spotty in the tunnels.

She dialed the general's number and waited.

"General Brushwood's office," the secretary answered.

"Hi, this is Katie. I was hoping to catch the general in his office."

"Katie who?"

"Just Katie," she replied happily. "He will know who I am."

"Please hold," the secretary replied abruptly.

Pandora snickered. *Someone needs to get laid.*

Right?

"Katie!" the general exclaimed. "Good to hear from you. How is everything going?"

"It's going really well," Katie replied. "I just got word that as of right now we are capable of producing four thousand rounds a day."

"That's *fantastic*."

"It is," Katie agreed. "What's even better is that very soon—and I mean days, not weeks—we will be up to twenty-five thousand a day."

"That's almost the only good news I've heard recently." He covered the receiver and coughed to the side, then returned to the conversation. "So what can I do for you?"

"Well, with production on that scale Charles will need people to help."

"How many do you need?"

"I was told that we will need seven people who can come in the morning, work, then leave in the evenings," Katie answered.

"That isn't a problem at all," the general replied. "I will call Nellis right after we hang up and have seven of their most trustworthy armaments specialists briefed and sent over to you first thing tomorrow."

"We need to make sure that they will keep what they see on this base a complete secret," Katie reminded him. "I don't have to tell you how fragile this whole situation is. We don't have a crew of armed guards protecting our base twenty-four hours a day and we're still a bit jumpy after the last attack."

"Understandable," the general agreed. "I can assure you that these men will be completely and totally discreet. They will comprehend the importance of secrecy, and if they don't I will handle it like I did Travis. How is he doing, by the way?"

"He seems to be doing very well." Katie chuckled. "He has fallen right in line, and is really bringing some good stuff to the table."

"Good. Maybe we scared him straight."

"Oh, and I have another thirty boxes of rounds for you," Katie said. "That's three thousand bullets so I hope that will keep you at least for a little while."

"Now that's the best news I've had in the last few days," the general exclaimed. "We needed more, but I figured it would be a while before we saw the next batch."

"To be honest, so did I," Katie replied. "I went over there today and Charles showed me what he had produced. I was blown away. I figured it would be weeks before we saw numbers like that. That's why I called you right away about the help. They are moving at lightspeed over here and I can't seem to keep up."

"That's a good thing, at least in your line of work. Luckily for you, you won't be taking any angry customer service calls over delays."

"I sure hope not." Katie sighed. "Stephanie is the customer service department and I don't know if she has that kind of patience."

"We will take care of that when the time comes," he replied. "I will get someone over there this afternoon to pick up the ammunition and deploy it to where it is needed most."

"Excellent! I will let Korbin know we will have a visitor shortly."

"Perfect," the general replied. "You guys are doing a hell of a job over there, that's for sure."

"Calls haven't come that often lately, so we've had that extra time to really get things under control," Katie explained. "I know you probably see more than we do since you have the whole country to look at, but around here it's been quiet. I think if we didn't have this to focus on we all might go a little stir-crazy."

"They're coming, don't you worry about that. It's just a question of when," the general assured her. "It looks like I have a call coming in from Tactics, so I am going to have to let you go."

"Not a problem. We'll get those bullets to your man."

"And Katie?" the general said before hanging up. "Thank you."

"You're welcome, General. We all want the same outcome. How we get there is just details."

They hung up and Katie sat there for a moment thinking about what had just been said. It was the first time the general had ever thanked her for anything.

Maybe the alliance wasn't such a bad idea after all. The teams needed a bigger force, more eyes, and a better ability to obtain the tools they needed for success, and the military were just the people to make sure that happened.

Her only concern was what it would all cost in the end.

Korbin was reviewing the newest intel.

Nothing much was different from what he had talked to the crew about earlier that day. Incursions were down in numbers, but the ones that *were* coming in were crazy-difficult.

The demons were getting smarter. Whoever was sending them their way knew they needed to up their game.

If they had upped their ante, the team had to as well.

That meant more training, longer hours, and new tactics, and though the teams were already being pushed, they were going to have to work even harder.

He hated to do that to them, but that was their job.

Korbin leaned back in the chair and rubbed his hands over his face, exhausted by all the changes. Something was going to have to give somewhere, because everything was running hot at that moment. Just then the phone rang and Korbin stared at it for a moment, almost too discouraged to pick it up.

"Korbin?" the general began. "It's Brushwood."

"General. How can I help you?"

"I just got off the phone with Katie ten minutes ago. There's a call in Wyoming and I'd like to know if I can have her and Damian. They would be the best people to take care of this situation since we don't know what we're facing."

"Sure. So there isn't much information on it yet?"

"No. It could be those damned mercenary demons again, or it could be just something simple." The general groaned. "But I don't want to find out the hard way and lose more good soldiers if I don't have to. Katie and

Damian can handle a hell of a lot more than these soldiers can, and if it's bad there will be more than enough reinforcements. If it's simple, they still won't have wasted a trip."

"Absolutely," Korbin agreed. "It's been quiet out here for a while now, which makes me nervous, but we're thankful that we got a bit of recovery time in."

"Katie told me," the general replied. "Hopefully this isn't a lead-up to something big."

"I'm hoping it's not as well. But yes, send me the info and I will get Damian and Katie geared up and ready to go. We have no time to waste."

"Oh, and in case Katie hasn't had a chance to tell you yet, I'm sending a man over to pick up ammunition this afternoon," the general told him.

"Not a problem," Korbin replied. "I will have the guys looking out for him. I'll alert Charles since Katie won't be here."

"Thank you, and I'll send that information over as soon as I can," he replied.

They hung up and Korbin went to the intercom. The speaker squealed loudly and he winced, waiting for the issue to resolve.

"Katie and Damian, report to my office as quickly as possible. You have a call."

Korbin walked back to the desk and pulled up the info from the general, printing a copy for them. Five minutes later they were in Korbin's office, breathing a bit harder than normal from jogging through the tunnels to get there quickly.

"What's up, boss?" Katie asked. "Local incursion?"

"Nope. The general called. Something's going on in Wyoming."

He handed the information to Katie.

"Wyoming?" Katie wrinkled her nose. "That's not our area."

"Yeah, and we don't really know what it is yet. We're just hoping it's not the demon mercs. They don't want to lose another band of soldiers by sending them into a trap."

"So, they called the professionals." Damian nodded. "Smart."

"Pretty much," Korbin replied. "I need you to leave as soon as you possibly can, so gear up and we'll ready the chopper."

"You got it, boss." Katie nodded and turned toward the door.

Korbin sighed and shook Damian's hand, knowing they were going into a dangerous situation.

He would have felt better sending the whole team, but emptying the base right then would not be wise. Without major security and with the presence of civilians they couldn't take the chance.

Katie and Damian headed for the armory and started packing. Katie was already wearing her specialty knives but she twisted her quarterstaff apart and shoved the halves into the leg holsters she'd had made. Damian nodded in approval and holstered his pistols at his sides. Katie knew she should be nervous. She knew this could be what had been bothering her for days, but nerves wouldn't do her any good at that point. It seemed like Pandora knew that too.

I am your inner Valium, she assured Katie. *Just take deep breaths. No one knows what this is, and I won't have a good idea until we get closer.*

Aye, aye, Captain, Katie replied.

"You ready?" Damian asked.

"As ready as I'll ever be, heading into a random incursion in a random place with no intel whatsoever," she replied.

"I know. We need a better system than this," Damian agreed. "If we had intel on every situation we might be able to cut the team, military, and civilian death rate in half."

"Big dreams." Katie smiled, throwing her bag over her shoulder. "We live in a world of big dreams."

"More like big nightmares." Damian scoffed and grabbed his bag and they headed out. "But hey, I'm gainfully employed."

"You don't really have much choice," Katie commented.

"Sure I do," Damian argued. "Death or lab rat are always available."

"You don't have another choice you would pick *voluntarily.*" She amended.

Worlds away in the fiery depths of hell, T'Chezz and Moloch sat in Moloch's office discussing the most recent attacks and where they would go next.

As always T'Chezz irritated Moloch, but where it used

to be a minor irritation it had now developed into full-blown loathing.

He kept his cool, though, knowing what they were doing was one for the books.

If worse came to worst and it all went south, he could pin the whole thing on T'Chezz and walk away scot-free. Lucifer would throw T'Chezz so far into the depths of hell if he fucked this up that he wouldn't see the topside lava for millennia. And if he *did* somehow crawl out, Moloch suspected Lucifer would toss him back for further baking.

"Our second success was just as I planned—*amazing*," T'Chezz boasted. "The team really has a handle on tactics now and they rolled in there ready to go. There were no survivors, or so I heard."

"Nope, no survivors." Moloch's teeth clenched with annoyance at the sound of T'Chezz's voice.

"I just wish they had been those Damned mercenaries and not idiot humans," T'Chezz lamented. "But like everything else, there is always room for improvement."

"Right," Moloch agreed through gritted fangs. "And we will get it right. I am sure of that. If nothing else, it was a good warmup for the main event. These men are training harder and longer than any other team and it shows when they roll into a battle. They are more than ready."

"Good," T'Chezz exclaimed. "Now what's for lunch?"

"I'm not sure," Moloch replied. "Why don't you make yourself comfortable and I will see what I can find out."

"Thank you."

As Moloch stalked out of his office and shut the door behind him, a low growl came from his snarling lips. As he walked through the building he ran into Baal and paused to chat. Moloch sighed, feeling everything bubbling over.

"How's it going?" Baal asked.

Moloch lost it.

"That idiot! That motherfucking idiot who can't even figure out which way his horns should go on in the morning has had the audacity to take credit, not only for what I am doing but for what generations of demons have laid the groundwork for us to achieve. He's a fucking lazy coward, and I want to snap his big fat scaly neck every time he opens his damn mouth."

"Why don't you just get rid of him," Baal asked. "You don't need him for this."

"He is the fall guy," Moloch growled, shaking his head. "I really need him to shut the fuck up, though."

"What happens if it succeeds?" Baal asked.

"Then I will cast him into the depths of hell myself." Moloch smirked evilly. "Either way, when this is all over I don't have to worry about that idiot making a mess of anything ever again. I will breathe easily at the top of the pack."

"Sometimes when you want something done you have to do it yourself," Baal remarked. "And you are getting to that point."

20

Timothy stood back and watched as the two women worked, impressed by their speed and accuracy. He was still bummed they weren't hot shirtless men, but he would have to deal with it.

At least his demon wasn't air-humping them or pushing him to stick his wang in either of them. They must not have been his type—although apparently *every* woman was his type, which Timothy found both desperate and gross.

He didn't care what anyone else did, but this demon was in *him*—and he was really tired of dreaming about man-eating vaginas.

"Okay." One of the women stood up and dusted off her hands. "That's it."

"That's it?" Calvin asked. "You're done?

"Yep. We locked and loaded all your servers, including OS updates and patches. Your firewall is locked down, and your connectivity is up and running, good as new."

"I'll be the judge of that," Timothy growled, turning to the computer and typing quickly.

Screens were popping up faster than Calvin had ever seen, but he wasn't sure what he was looking for.

Timothy kept typing, clicking through pages, updating settings, and looking through all the work the girls had done. They stood there smirking, confident in the work they had done.

When he was finished he turned around and nodded.

"Nice work, ladies. We are good to go."

"Thanks," The other one said, slinging her bag over her shoulder. "Whoever did this before was a bit of an idiot."

"Yeah." The other scoffed. "Whoever they were, they didn't even connect the firewall correctly."

"Psst!" Timothy slid his hand across his neck to tell them to shut up.

Calvin cleared his throat and crossed his arms over his chest.

"The person who did *that*," he pointed to the machines, "was killed in a gang fight when we were working with the police," Calvin explained. "He was protecting innocent civilians and the rest of the city from falling into these mad men's grasp. It would be good of you to show a bit of respect."

"You're right," one girl agreed, hanging her head. "That was catty."

"It was," the other chimed in. "We had no idea, but that isn't an excuse. Sorry about that."

"No problem." Calvin eased up.

"Just don't let the chick in spandex hear that." Timothy rolled his eyes. "She's a snippy one."

He raked his hand through the air like a cat and made a hissing noise. The girls stifled their laughs and looked at Calvin, who stomped forward, scaring Timothy.

"Come on, ladies, I'll show you the way out." He motioned toward the door and turned to Timothy. "And *you* better stay out of trouble while I am gone. There is nowhere you can go that I won't find you."

"Not moving a muscle," Timothy replied.

Calvin walked out of the room and took the lead to make sure they didn't make any wrong turns. He took them the long way through the tunnels to avoid walking past occupied rooms.

They went up the elevator and to their car, where he handed each of them an envelope of cash and a case of PBR. He shook his head when they got more excited about the beer than the money and watched until they had driven out of sight.

"Fucking white people," he grumbled, getting back into the elevator.

When he got back to the room Timothy was typing feverishly and papers were falling out of the printer. Calvin picked one up and read it. It was intel—data streams—and only some of it made sense to him.

"What is this?" he asked, holding up a page. "What are you doing right now?"

"I am pulling in information, and data; everything I can get my hands on," Timothy told him excitedly. "I'm implementing a few butler programs as well. This hardware is amazing quality. I have to admit I'm impressed, now that it is up and running."

Calvin just stared at him, concerned that Timothy was

doing something he shouldn't, but Calvin couldn't tell. "What's a butler program?"

"It's a program that a lot of hackers use," he explained, still typing. "In simple terms, it's a smart script that grabs the input and works to make my life easier as we hack for information. Basically, the system—Siebel in this case—is asking one user questions and getting the answers from another. Sometimes it is user-to-user, as in the same person, but for obvious reasons that doesn't do much."

"Like the fact that I can't ask myself a question I don't know the answer to and get a response?" Calvin asked.

"Kind of, but in a much more technical and complicated way," he replied. "When I'm hacking, it helps if I know the answers before I get there so I can breeze through whatever it is I am working on."

"Okaayyy," Calvin agreed slowly. "And how will any of this help us?"

"It's information." He shrugged. "It's what you people call 'intel.' I might have to spell some of it out for you here and there, but it's going to help you do whatever it is you guys actually do…besides torturing the poor gay tech guy."

"No one is torturing you," Calvin grumbled. "*Yet*."

Timothy swallowed hard but acted like he hadn't heard Calvin's comment.

He was used to being treated a certain way. He was a weirdo by society's standards, but he had learned to live with that. He got back at society through its computers.

It was really the only thing he knew how to do. Calvin walked over to the phone and called Korbin.

"Korbin, come down to the server room. I want to show you something."

"Uh-oh, calling in the big dog," Timothy joked.

"He should see this. Time is of the essence," Calvin explained, turning as Korbin entered the room.

Korbin's eyes widened when he saw all the paper and flashing lights. "Wow, looks like things are up and running!"

"Timothy is pulling all kinds of information off... Well, wherever the hell he pulls it from," Calvin told him. "I figured you would want to know."

"I do," Korbin agreed, walking over to Timothy. "Let me ask you a question: is this system capable of tracking people down?"

"Sure. I would just need some sort of reference point," he replied.

"I have surveillance footage, and I want to know who the people in it are."

"Oh, yeah." Timothy nodded. "That will be pretty easy. I can just cross-hack into the police systems and start there. I can use their facial recognition software and get hundreds of answers within minutes. I mean, I have to hack into them first, but after that it'll be a breeze."

"All right. Good." Korbin handed him a flash drive. "It's on here, but you need to know that it's top secret. I just want the identities of the men in that video."

"There you go again, being more than prepared," Timothy teased, taking the thumb drive. "I'll get started on it right now."

"Good," Korbin said. "Report to me as soon as you know any of their names."

"Got it," he replied. "Do you want me to call you on that

old-ass intercom," he jerked his thumb over his shoulder, "or tell my giant bodyguard about it?"

"Tell Calvin." Korbin grinned. "He will contact me immediately. In the meantime, continue to collect intel on the groups listed in the documents on the drive. We want as much intel as we can get. Things are starting to heat up, and we don't want to be in the dark."

"You want me to stay here, boss?" Calvin asked.

"I know it's not the most glamorous assignment, but yes," Korbin replied. "Until we can trust this one on his own, we will need someone watching him. When he gets tired, his room has been set up. It's two doors down from yours. I will send someone to relieve you eventually. Katie and Damian are on their way to a fight out in Wyoming."

"Wyoming?" Calvin asked, looking shocked. "What the hell are they doing out there?"

"Taking in the buffalo, chillin' on the ranch, eating some ranchers," Timothy quipped, not looking at them.

"We aren't really sure," Korbin replied, ignoring Timothy. "There was no intel on it when they left. The general called down and asked for the two of them specifically. I guess we just have to wait and see."

"Right, well, tell me as soon as you know something," Calvin requested. "Things are getting much worse out there."

The jet's wheels touched lightly down on the runway and the pilot applied the brakes, slowing it way down as he taxied toward the hangar bay in front of him. Other planes lifted off and landed, all military. Once again they were the only ones in a private plane.

Katie took a deep breath and nodded at Damian as they taxied, standing up and tugging on her gear once they had stopped completely to make sure it was secure.

Damian picked his cross up off the table beside him and tucked it into his inside jacket pocket.

When the two exited the plane there were a men standing guard with M-16s in hand. They went to the cargo hold and pulled out their bags, slinging them over their shoulders.

The scene wasn't playful, as it had been the other times Katie had landed at a base. Even the guards kept their eyes straight ahead and their bodies rigidly attentive. Immediately her anxiety began to return, but she had known it would. She was always anxious before a fight.

She just needed to focus and get into the right frame of mind.

What the hell? Pandora bitched. *No one is checking you out. I tightened, toned, and lifted everything before we left and not a single eye has moved over this luscious booty. I'm missing the sausage something awful.*

Hmm? Katie said not paying attention. *I'm not really fond of sausage. This isn't the right time for food, though.*

Pandora scoffed. *Wake up, zombie bride. I wasn't talking about links or patties. You know, the guy's tool? His big salami? Willy the Wonder Worm? Tube Snake? No? How about Baloney Pony, Chicksicle, Bed Snake, or in regard to Calvin, Alabama Black Snake. Hello? Earthworm Jim, Fat Albert, Grabthar's Hammer, Otis Deepthroatis? Ferchrissake, are you alive out there? I have given you more than a dozen alternative names for*

Herman von Longschlongenstein and you are still in another world.

Herman von what? Katie finally said. *Kajesus, Pandora, just how many code names do you have for it?*

At least a thousand. She considered. *Occasionally they are old references and at least thirty are probably extinct languages, but the point is the same, really. Need I continue? Tan Banana, Thrill Drill...*

No! Katie whimpered in exhaustion. *Please do not go on. I know what you are talking about. I'm sorry you miss the D.*

"The D?" Pandora repeated. *Gonna add that one to the list.*

Pandora, I'm a little preoccupied at the moment. I'm walking into a fight with no idea what I am going to find and a possible demon mercenary team on my heels, Katie snapped angrily. *And all my demon can talk about is some guys getting a piece of ass—specifically mine. I'm glad none of them are checking me out. I have no time for that today.*

Sheesh, calm down! You need to relax a bit. Pandora scoffed. *I'm just tooled up because no one enjoyed my efforts. Damn, need more of* something.

Damian put his hand out, drawing Katie's attention back. The two stopped and set their bags on the ground as a tall officer with a serious face and a perfect uniform approached. The shadow from his hat covered his eyes, and if it weren't for the fact that when he raised the brim they were baby blue, Katie might have suspected he was one of *them.* When he reached them he took off his hat and held it under his arm. He crossed his hands in front of him and nodded at both Katie and Damian.

"Thank you for getting here so fast," he began. "You must be Katie."

"That's me," she said.

"Father." He turned to Damian and nodded.

"I'm Colonel Ambrose, the team leader for the Black Squad," he continued. "We are a special division of the 173rd Infantry. We are highly classified and considered black ops. We will be working with you today on this incursion."

"Nice to meet you," Damian replied. "Have we gotten any more information about what we might be walking into?"

"A little," he said. "You got here at the perfect time. The team is assembling inside the main building to go over the ops report. That will begin in ten minutes. Your timing couldn't have been better, at least for us. We were given a go by our command as the wheels of your jet touched down on the runway, which is why I wasn't waiting for you. My apologies."

"No problem," Katie assured him. "Where can we put our gear?"

"Right this way," he replied, putting on his hat and turning around sharply.

Katie glanced at Damian, who took a deep breath before following the colonel.

She gritted her teeth as they left the hangar and went down a long hallway to a door with a passcode. They waited for Ambrose to plug in the code and open the door before following him.

They walked past the weapons checkpoint and down another long corridor to a meeting room with rows of chairs. The men milling around inside stopped, then sat down as Ambrose pointed to the row in front.

"Those are *your* seats," he told them. "But you can put your bags over here. Take whatever you think you'll need when we leave. Anything else can stay in this room. It will be secured at all times while you are away."

"Thank you," Damian replied, putting his bag down. "We tend not to overpack in situations like this. We have our essentials."

"Perfect."

Katie put her bag down next to Damian's and they walked to their seats, She felt the soldier's eyes on her. She cleared her throat and sat down, crossing her legs and clutching her knee.

Back in the game, Pandora cheered.

Katie rolled her eyes and kept her thoughts to herself.

"Set everything up in the center of the room," Trenton ordered, pointing with his right hand. "I want this to go *smoothly.*"

One of the victims in the group whimpered through the cloth tied around her mouth. Trenton tilted his head to the side and ran his finger down her cheek. He shushed her using a calming melodic tone.

"Don't cry," he told her, his voice comforting. "Our master will be here soon..." he nodded, eyes sympathetic, "and he will have you as his afternoon snack."

Trenton's eyes lit up and he laughed in a deep tone.

The woman thrashed from side to side, screaming through her gag, as one of the mercenaries pulled her back into the group and sat her down hard on her ass. The others were racing around the room, setting up candles, lighting them, and drawing the appropriate symbols on the carpeted floors of the old hotel.

Trenton walked over to the window and pulled the

curtain back slightly, staring out at the mountainous terrain. He snickered at the thought of the invasion and how he would soon be ripping human heads from their shoulders.

When he turned back around, the area had been transformed into something like a deep old dungeon in a European castle.

Trenton smiled and rubbed his hands together as he scanned his troops, who were lined up at attention. As he walked along the line he stared down at each, his eyes bright red in the dark room.

"You have all done well today." He winked at the woman. "We were able to catch our victims efficiently, and now they will be a sacrifice to Moloch while sending a signal to the military. Once they determine where we are they will attack, which is when we bring the pain. Keep your heads at all times, both literally and metaphorically. I want no casualties on our side, but I want every single one of those military bitches to lie in a pool of their own blood by the time we are finished here. Moloch will let us know when they're coming, and I expect every single one of you to be more than prepared to jump into action. This is another day of reckoning for these humans. We *will* let them know just how far they have fallen."

He looked around with glowing red eyes and beat a fist on his chest. "It is *our* day and we *WILL NOT FAIL.*"

"Soldiers," Ambrose began, addressing the group in the room. "We have been called on another mission, this one close to our hearts. The same group suspected of killing our brothers and sisters just weeks ago is now believed to be setting up in a hotel in the mountains not far from here. Our mission is to go in, kill whatever demon scum we find, and leave unscathed. To help us in this mission we have two of the most successful mercenaries on the teams, Katie and Damian. They will be the first in and will be our eyes and ears before we get there. Katie will be heading things up and will tell us when we have reached our destination. When we are with them we treat them as our own. From what the general has described, these two will be *invaluable* to us."

The colonel picked up a sheet of paper from the table. Katie could see a strain on his face and she knew there was more. He sighed and stepped forward again, looking out over the soldiers.

"The people responsible for this have abducted a group of innocents," he continued. "Foul play is to be expected, since this isn't their first rodeo. Those innocents are now our responsibility as well, and I want to see as many of them as possible brought back from harm. It will be dark, it will be dangerous, and demons are hard to spot, but trust our leaders and trust your instincts. If you think they are innocent, check their eyes for the red rings. If clear, it is your job to get them to safety. This is a 'no shit' situation as in 'no shit, this is dangerous.' We will move these people out, but also need to have eyes in the back of our heads. Look out for each other. Make sure we take down as many of these demon mercs as possible. They *cannot* continue killing our brothers and sisters, hunting our allies, and murdering the innocent of this country. Any questions?"

A red-haired guy raised his hand and nodded toward the two in the front. "Will Katie and Damian be fighting with us?"

"We will," Katie answered, then blushed, realizing she had spoken out of turn. She looked at the colonel and raised an eyebrow, but he nodded back so she continued, "We are on your team now, and will do everything we can to keep as many safe as possible. We were called in by the general to help reduce casualties on our side and increase them on theirs. That is what he expects of us." She made a wry face, "And you know how much generals love to be disappointed." There were a few chuckles from the group.

The phone behind her rang and the colonel answered, keeping his voice low.

"We want you to have one-hundred-percent faith that we are on your side," Katie continued. "We will enter the facility first and assess, taking down as many as we can to make your entrance smoother. Once we determine their strength we will let you know exactly where we need you to set up."

"Thank you," the colonel said. "That was General Brushwood at the main command. There was a massive interdimensional surge in the general area of the mountains, which confirms the presence of a higher demon. The sheriff and the police have been ordered to stand down and move back. During this incursion we will be implementing a new weapon, something that has the power to turn the tide if the battle is going poorly. Katie, would you mind explaining the bullets?"

"Sure." Katie stood up and stepped over to join the colonel. "You will all be given a ration of rounds. These rounds are to be loaded into your weapons exclusively. They can impair and even kill demons. With enough hits, even the largest ones will go down. There is a specific metal in them that poisons demons when it comes in contact with their bodies, incapacitating them for a short period. These bullets work like any others, except with these if you shoot a demon in the head most of them will die. But they also buy you time in a close situation if you hit them anywhere. Use them sparingly, and please..." she smiled, but it failed to reach her eyes, "watch your aim around Damian and me. We may have demons in us, but I promise we are the good guys."

Katie then produced a real smile and gave the floor back to Ambrose. She sat down in the chair and let out a deep breath, curious as to what the soldiers thought about their presence.

She knew it had to be confusing to fight alongside the very thing they were tasked to take down, but this alliance could bring them a reprieve.

She looked at those men like she did the innocents: they were her responsibility to keep safe. She feared, though, they saw her and Damian differently.

Only time would tell how they truly felt.

"It is time." Trenton stood in the center of the circle of men and raised his hands.

One of the mercs grabbed the woman by the hair and

threw her into the circle. Trenton smiled and shushed her once again, then flipped her around and held her with one hand as he raised a knife high with the other. He cracked his neck and closed his eyes, ready to summon the high demon Moloch.

"*Ozz mighty Moloch, la summon esaeu mnaez ya depths aem sazz,*" Trenton called in the demon language. "*La sowa xnaeuksq o mighty bounty maen esaeun k'aozuna. Baeir uz aes knaoq aera!*"

Trenton continued to hold the knife in the air as the others chanted loudly, then lowered the knife to the woman's throat, gripping her tightly against him. He growled, his eyes growing brighter by the second.

"*Baeir uz aes knaoq aera!*"

With that he sliced the woman's throat and released her, and she collapsed to the ground, the deep red of her claret darkening the dirty carpet beneath her.

Trenton raised the knife to his lips and ran his tongue across it, savoring her blood. He breathed deeply as wind began to blow wildly through the room.

A shudder shook the walls and pictures crashed to the floor around them, then a beam of red light brightened the space as Moloch stepped out and gently floated to the ground.

Screams of terror erupted from the victims as two of them were stabbed repeatedly before their bodies were thrown down for Moloch's delight. He picked up the woman's body and licked the blood from her neck, groaning in ecstasy and relishing the cacophony of fear and pain exuded by those around him.

This was the ecstasy that orgasmed in his brain,

sending his desire to rip and tear into a frenzy. However, as one of the Eight, he was the master of the emotions.

If not his demonic desires.

Trenton stepped back and watched as Moloch devoured the woman in front of him, leaving not even a sliver of flesh at his feet.

Moloch grabbed the bodies in his gigantic black paws and waving his hand. A carved door appeared, and he flung it open, revealing nothing but darkness and screams on the other side.

Before he stepped through he turned to Trenton. "They're coming, so be careful."

The door slammed shut and the wind immediately ceased. Everyone let out a deep breath, their spirits and demons emboldened by the appearance of their master.

Each stood taller and felt stronger than they had a moment before.

Their eyes now glowed bright red like Trenton's. The leader sheathed his knife and stepped before the men.

"See what comes of our everlasting faith?" he yelled. "Our master has come and given us his blessing. The soldiers are approaching, and now it is your job to show Moloch what we are made of. Remind him of our usefulness, our loyalty, and our *dedication* to the death of the unEnlightened!"

Moloch walked through the door to his home dimension and sat down hard on a large stone, dropping the two bodies in front of him. He growled as he lifted one and took a bite, then wiped his bloody mouth on his arm. He looked at Baal, who was sitting to his left with his back against the stone and puffing on a large cigar.

"So, how did it go?" Baal asked with a smirk.

"Stupid humans." Moloch chuckled. "They really think I am their god. They will walk through fire for me, even if it burns every last inch of their flesh off their bones. All I have to do is say the word. I now understand why Lucifer loves to be Lucifer. To be in command of so many, able to move them at your will… It's *more* than exhilarating."

"Be careful," Baal cautioned, removing the cigar from his black lips and using it to point to Moloch. "You don't want all that power to go to your head. Lucifer will *always* be the king."

"But to be next to him, to be his left hand—or his right, or anything in his line of sight—would give me so much power," Moloch replied. "Today, though, we push on, moving toward collecting more human bodies, shedding more innocent blood, and laughing in the faces of those who scream in terror."

"Sounds exciting." Baal chuckled and snapped a limb off one of the humans.

Moloch slapped Baal's hand and growled at him. "Go to Earth and get your own snacks."

"You need a vacation." Baal waved him off with a frown. "This takeover has made you even grumpier than you were before."

K atie stared out of the helicopter's windows, looking at the other chopper carrying the soldiers.

She and Damian rode alone as first-in. They didn't want to take the chance of landing with the men and facing an ambush before they could settle the tactics to be used for the mission.

Her headset was connected to the other chopper so she could converse with Ambrose when the time was right. Katie tapped the pilot on the shoulder as they crossed into the mountains.

"I want you to make a loop." She waved her finger in a circle. "Fly around the mountains."

The pilot gave her the thumbs-up as he spoke into his microphone to the other pilot. The other helicopter followed them, close enough to keep radio contact but far enough behind to get out of the way if they needed to.

Katie stared down at the canopy of trees below, using

Pandora to track the area for any sign of demons. The moon was full in the sky and it lit the forest just enough to see the winding road below them.

There was no one traveling the lonely forest, which was good since they didn't need *more* innocents involved.

The chopper made several loops through the mountains and slowly approached an abandoned hotel high on a slope. Katie felt that same tingle in the pit of her stomach she had been feeling for days.

She wasn't sure if it was a sign or because the place looked like something straight out of a horror film.

The courtyards were overgrown, shingles were missing, and the windows were dark and ominous.

That's it, Pandora told her. *They are in the hotel.*

Of course they are, Katie groaned.

"I want everyone to land in that open area above the hotel," Katie instructed the pilot.

He nodded and instructed the other pilot to follow him down.

When they landed Katie and Damian got out of their chopper and grabbed what they needed from their bags. They headed over to the soldiers, who had lined up in front of the colonel to await further instruction.

The choppers took off and headed back to the base.

"They're in the hotel," Katie told the group as she walked up. "I can't tell how many there are, but with a surge of energy like the one witnessed by the general, there is—or at least *was*—a high-level and dangerous demon here."

"What's the plan?" the colonel asked.

"Damian and I will enter first and alone." She looked

around. "You and your men will make a circle around the hotel. That way if any of these rats try to escape, they are trapped."

Katie turned to the troops and addressed them directly. "Remember, use the ammo I gave you. If they are the demon mercs, the bullets will mess them up like nothing you've seen. If you run out of the special bullets team up— use one of the special rounds to mess the demon up and then shoot the fucker right between the eyes with the regular round. That should do the trick. We will try to keep them contained, but again...we don't know how many we are facing or what weapons they have. They have the same powers as the mercenary teams you have now allied with, so this will not be a normal fight for any of us. As soon as we have secured the hotel we will let you know on the comm. Good luck, do your best, and I hope we all see each other when this is over."

Katie drew the colonel to the side as she adjusted her gear. She pulled out her pistol and held it tightly in her hand, looking down at the ground. Her emotions were unlike her; she felt for the men, and she could already recognize every single one of their faces. She wasn't sure why she felt this way, but she had to make sure they stayed safe.

"Be smart out there," she told the colonel. "Protect these men. If Damian and I are killed, don't be heroes. Get your men the hell out of here. If *we* can't take them, your team will die in seconds."

He frowned before blowing out a breath. "Understood. And thank you."

"You're welcome." Katie smiled kindly. "We'll see you on the flip side, wherever that may be."

Katie caught up with Damian at the edge of the woods and they started toward the hotel looming in the distance. They walked silently for several moments, gathering their thoughts and focusing on getting to the hotel in one piece.

"You are awfully sentimental today," Damian remarked.

"I know," Katie replied. "It's gross. I don't like it. Something must be wrong with me."

"You're human." Damian chuckled.

Pandora snickered. *That's* definitely *what's wrong with you.*

You keep your comments to yourself, Katie snapped.

Snippy. Pandora scoffed. *And I know it's not your period since I took care of that shit.*

"It's okay to care about these men," Damian told her. "You have lost a lot recently and it has made you—"

"Softer?" Katie cut him off. "I just want this to be successful, that's all. Now, if you are done with the heart-to-heart, we have some demons to slay."

They stared at the hotel with lumps in their throats.

The demon mercs pulled the remaining hostages into the foyer and shoved them together, then circled them with rope and twisted until none of them could move so much as an inch.

One of the higher-ups in the group pulled a small box from his bag and attached it to the ropes, lifting the lid and pressing some buttons. The lights began to flash and he stepped back with a smile.

They had been bound with a wireless explosive.

"All right team, huddle up over here," Trenton called. "They are close; I can smell them. It's not smart for us to stay in one group. That could cause more casualties. I want us to split up into two teams—half go with Ryan, the other half with me. We are looking for mercenaries; we never know when they could be involved. This is a high-level incursion, so they should have called the teams. When you find them, hold off killing them. I want to talk to them first. The rest of the soldiers are yours for the taking."

Trenton looked down at the blueprint of the hotel he had spread out on a side table. He drew his finger along the passages, trying to find the best route. He looked out the window and shook his head.

"Brian, Eli, you are two of our best, and frankly, I trust you to not fuck up." Trenton looked out a nearby window. "I am sending you out into the field to hide. I want you to sneak up behind whoever is heading in and cut their legs off before they get here."

"Yes, sir!"

"Be careful out there. You don't want to become the victim of your own plan," Trenton instructed. "The rest of us will settle down here and wait for your signal. Use guns so we can hear the shots. If you need us we will come to you, but if you can't kill them try to push them inside to us. They will want to save the innocents, but really they are out for revenge whether or not they want to admit it. They will want to find us, and we will be more than happy to greet them at the door."

Both men nodded and Trenton stepped to the side as they made their way out the door.

He shut it behind them and turned back to the troops. He could tell they were nervous. The last thing he needed was a bunch of trigger-happy anxious soldiers.

He put up his hands. "Everyone settle down. There is no reason to be nervous. Moloch came to us, which means he supports this mission. I want you to spread out across this area and hunker down with your weapons at the ready. We kicked the last team's asses without effort, and there is no reason that we won't do the same with this one. You are ready. Talk to your demons and summon your strength. We are in for a battle."

The soldiers spread out across the large marbled foyer, taking a knee and watching out the large windows. Trenton backed up to the hostages and snickered as he petted one of them on the cheek. The fear in her eyes made him smile.

"It will all be over soon, sweetie. Don't worry."

Katie and Damian circled around the hotel to the front, figuring the best thing to do was walk straight in the front doors and face the sonsabitches head-on. They crouched at the edge of the woods for a moment, then stepped forward.

Wait, Pandora warned. *There are two demon mercs stalking you.*

Katie put her hand out and stopped Damian, pulling him close to her. She didn't know where the demons were or if they could hear her, so she spoke just above a whisper.

"I need you to back me up. There are two demons behind us, Pandora is sniffing out their exact location. I am going to swing around and get them from behind."

"Got it," Damian whispered.

Katie carefully moved to the right and disappeared quickly behind a tree. She looked into the woods to her left, letting Pandora guide her sight to one of the two. He was crouched behind a tree and was staring at the hotel.

He apparently hadn't spotted her yet, so she snuck up behind him and covered his mouth with her hand. She pulled her knife from her vest and slowly slit his throat, sensing the enraged demon screaming inside him. His blood spilled onto the soil as he fell to the ground.

Katie wiped her knife on his shirt and looked around for the other. Suddenly his communication device clicked, and Katie smirked down at it. She picked it up and raised it to her mouth, but instead of her voice speaking it was Pandora's.

"One down, my little imps," she purred. "Momma's here —and she's not playing."

Katie snorted. *Cute.*

It's all in the theatrics, Pandora replied.

As the soldiers listened to Pandora's voice over their earpieces, Trenton gritted his teeth and clenched his hands into fists. A moment later a shrill scream echoed through the woods and into the hotel.

Trenton pressed his finger against his earpiece.

"That's two down," the voice informed them. "Looks like I'll be feasting on the entrails of the stupid today."

"Goddammit," Trenton yelled as he stood up. "That *bitch*."

The soldiers didn't move. They just sat there staring at Trenton, unsure what to do next.

Trenton was furious, and so dumbfounded by the fact he had already lost two men that rage blazed through him.

He looked at the soldiers, then went over to the innocents and growled in their terrified faces.

"I am going to personally make this bitch pay," he whispered. "She is *mine*, and if anyone finds her first, bring her ass to *me*. The games are over. It's time for these bastards to meet their bloody ends."

23

From a distance, you wouldn't be able to see the military carefully creating a circle around the hotel.

They looked like ants lining up to protect their queen.

Ready for battle, ready to get revenge for their fallen brothers and sisters.

None of them liked to be pushed to the back, but they understood that the mercenaries were their allies, and that if anything, they were taking the brunt of the blows from whatever demons were inside.

They were the tanks.

The colonel split the men into two groups, sending one group to the other side and stopping his at the tree line.

They sat silently for several minutes, watching every door and every window, then suddenly there was a loud scream and the sound of a body hitting the ground.

"Spread outward," the colonel instructed over the

comm. "Go slowly and cover the front of the hotel. Stay in the trees and report anything unusual."

"Copy," one of the soldiers replied.

He spied Damian crouched in the tall weeds and grasses, and there was movement on the edge of the woods so he raised his rifle. After he peered through the scope he lowered it again, though, since it was Katie walking out of the bushes with her hands covered in blood.

"Colonel, we have a body," the soldier called over the comm. "Wait, make that two. Two bodies, heavily armed."

"Copy that," the colonel replied. "Stay in ranks and keep your heads down. Katie took them out, so they must have been the enemy. Watch your backs. We don't know how many more are out here."

Ambrose switched the channel on his comm and clicked the button. "Katie, come in."

"I hear you, Colonel," she replied.

"We found two bodies. Want to confirm they were your kills."

"They were mine," she whispered. "They were demon mercs. I think we have a whole crew of them hunkered down inside. Hold your positions and don't let any of them get away."

"Copy that," the colonel replied, switching his channel back and calling the troops. "Demon mercs. Two down, unknown number inside."

"Copy that," the soldiers replied.

"Did you hear that scream?" one of the soldiers whispered. "He sounded like a fucking pig dying."

Another snickered. "Or a demon motherfucker meeting

his match. That chick is obviously not someone to be messed with."

"Damn straight," the first replied. "And she is sexy as hell, too."

"Careful now," Ambrose whispered. "You just might lose a finger if you try anything."

The soldier to his right laughed. "Or worse."

They sat there in the wood line watching as Katie and Damian disappeared into a small woodshed on the edge of the property.

Everything was silent; no bird calls, no insects—not even the sound of a plane flying overhead. It was eerie in a way that made the colonel's skin crawl.

They had one hell of a fight on their hands, and they could only hope the mercenaries did some damage before they had to fire a shot.

———

Katie carefully shut the woodshed door and crouched next to Damian, checking the bullets in her gun for the tenth time. She was nervous, but this time it wasn't because she was hunting demons. Damian peeked through a small hole in the side of the shed, but there was no movement outside.

"Are the rest of the demons inside?" Damian whispered.

"Yeah." Katie nodded. "They only sent the two out here. Idiots."

"You ready to go in?" Damian asked, moving toward the door.

"Wait. Turn off your comm for a second."

"All right." He looked at her with curiosity and switched off his comm. "What's going on?"

"I can't really explain this to you until it's a go," she began. "I need you to trust Pandora and me, though. Can you do that?" She looked him square in the eyes, seeking something.

"Yeah, of course," he replied, one eyebrow raised. "But I think that—"

Damian stopped talking and backed up slightly.

He watched as Katie shut her eyes, took a deep breath, and slowly let it out. Her head twisted and her movements were so fast that all he could see was a blur of her face. He put his hand on the butt of his pistol and watched carefully, unsure what the hell was going on.

He had told her that he trusted her and he meant it, so he left his gun in its holster. As her head movements slowed she rolled her neck, groaning quietly. Her features changed and she morphed into an even more voluptuous woman right in front of him.

His eyes grew wider and scanned her body as it too began to shake wildly.

He scooted back until his back was pressed against the door to the shed. He had never seen anything like it. Not only had her face changed, but so had her body; everything had been emphasized.

Her breasts were huge, her waist was tiny, and her hips were wide and curvaceous. Her eyes glowed red, matching her plump pouty lips.

Slowly the woman in front of him stood up and stretched her arms over her head as she yawned.

Damian blinked hard, unsure whether this was actually

happening or if he had stepped on something poisonous and was hallucinating the entire thing.

He tilted his head to the side as the hair flowed over her shoulders. When she opened her eyes again and looked at Damian, the red had simmered to a dull glow.

Her lips slowly curved into a smile and he wasn't sure whether to run, shoot, hump her, or stay exactly where he was.

Where had that desire to hump her come from?

He had been with the Damned longer than most, and things just kept getting weirder every time he turned around.

This, though…this took the cake.

The Katie he knew, the one he'd fought beside, worked beside, and played beside was gone.

Her features had changed and her body had been reshaped; there was nothing left of the woman he had grown to know so well.

In her place was another person, one he could only assume was the legend and the voice behind Katie's sweet face— Pandora, the demon inside her.

Damian had always wondered what she would look like in the flesh, but that wasn't at all how he had pictured her.

She was hot; hotter than any woman he had met. The entire thing was completely insane to him. He took his hand off his gun and slowly stood. Once he was up he stayed where he was, almost wanting to pinch himself to make sure he wasn't dreaming.

He reached down to flip his comm back on but stopped, wanting to figure out what the hell was going on first.

He couldn't talk though; words just didn't seem to want to form on his lips. He just stood there gaping at Pandora.

She sneered at him, then snickered and walked toward him, staring at Damian with excitement.

"Close your mouth, kitten," she suggested, gently pushing his mouth closed.

He blinked again, still not moving a muscle, completely stunned by the woman standing in front of him.

He wasn't sure if it was because she had morphed from one form to another or if it was because she was *stunningly* gorgeous.

He couldn't imagine this woman shoving so many donuts into her mouth or eating until Katie couldn't move anymore.

She was a supermodel, but at the same time, she was a demon through and through. And not just any demon—a very *very* powerful one.

When she took over a body it wasn't a disgusting beast. It was a totally different person.

"You know, you should stop looking at me like that," she purred, running her finger over his cheek. "Katie would be pissed if I made you break your sacred vows."

"But you… And there was Katie, and..." Damian shook his head and finally turned his eyes away.

He reached up and rubbed his face, then looked back at her as if she would magically become Katie again. She laughed and twirled around, letting out a deep breath.

"It feels so good to have a body again, even if it's only for a night," she exclaimed excitedly. "I feel like Cinderella with her pumpkin coach, only when this fight's over I'll turn back into Katie and sink back into the depths of her soul. So sad. At least tomorrow she can get me some more donuts and it will only affect her and not me. I like big hips, but not the kind I would have if I ate like that all the time. Even we demons are susceptible to fat thighs."

"What is going *on*?" Damian finally asked, shaking his head. "One minute Katie is here, and the next minute poof! Her demon is standing in front of me in the flesh. This shit *doesn't make any sense.*"

"Neat, huh?" Pandora smiled at Damian. "The truth is, she and I have wanted to try this for a while, but we never quite found the right time. Out here with you, we figured we could give this new trick a test run and see if it worked. So far so good in my opinion, though I'm not sure how Katie feels about it. I'm sure she will more than let me know later on when things get back to normal. For now, though," she waved a hand up and down her voluptuous body, "this is what just jumped out of the magic hat."

"Why is this necessary?" Damian asked. "Katie with your help is stronger than any other team member out there."

"Oh, sure," Pandora agreed, scrunching her nose as she looked around the old woodshed. "The thing is, she may be powerful, but not nearly powerful enough to beat my brother T'Chezz—or at least that was our consensus. So we decided to try this on for size, seeing if I could tap into her abilities if I completely and totally took over her body. Basically we flipped the script: instead of me being inside aiding her, she is inside and I am using my full powers and tapping into her natural ones—or at least that is how it is supposed to go." She shrugged. "We will see."

"Can all demons do this or just powerful ones like you?"

Pandora cocked her head. "Well, I suppose they all can do it to a certain extent, but usually when they are less powerful you get that weird-demon-with-the-droopy-human-suit thing going on. Then they vanish, and just the human is left. She and I, on the other hand, are tied together, and I am capable of completely transforming into myself. I have to admit, I've never done anything like it before. We didn't even know if it would work, but I think it's because Katie is special as much as because I'm powerful. This just might be a really good alternative to fighting, at least some of the time. We will have to wait and see how Katie's human body takes it."

"So if you're here, where is Katie?"

"Same place *I* usually am, I suppose."

"Can Katie come back out whenever she wants?"

"No." Pandora shook her head. "It's all based on trust now, little priest. She gave me permission and opened herself up for me to take her. For her to come back I have to will it so. But don't worry, I have every intention of bringing her back. This is a little uncomfortable. Now, there are a shit-ton of demon mercs in that hotel who are currently spreading out and hiding in all the nooks and crannies." Her eyes flashed and her lips curved into a luscious hungry smile. *"Let's go hunting."*

24

P andora and Damian left the woodshed and made their way to the front door of the hotel. Damian shielded her from those in the woods, hoping like hell none of them noticed the change.

From a distance Pandora looked enough like Katie to pass for her, but up close everyone would know it wasn't her.

Pandora sniffed the air outside the door and nodded.

"They have all hidden from me." Pandora smirked. "I have always liked a good game of hide-and-seek. Inside this door, you are going to find a group of humans tied together with explosive rope with a wireless trigger device. Get them untied and send them out toward the soldiers. I'm going to hunt those little fuckers down."

Damian stared at her for a moment, blinking hard. He still couldn't believe he was standing next to Katie's demon. She snapped her fingers in front of his face and patted him on the arm.

"Come on, priesty, stay with me," she urged. "I know it's a lot to take in, but you can stare later."

"Right. He shook his head. "Untie the humans and get them out of here. Got it."

Pandora pushed the door open and put her hand on Damian's chest, holding him back for a moment. She slowly pulled the short sword from her back and shoved it through the door, then snickered as a man gave a surprised grunt of pain.

She pulled her bloody sword back out and put it back into its sheath, stepping over the body on the floor as she entered.

Damian lifted one eyebrow and shook his head, then followed her into the foyer. He went to work untying the humans while Pandora wandered off into the rest of the hotel.

She crept down a hallway with a smirk on her face. She passed a closed door, then stopped and turned back sharply, whipping her hair over her shoulder. She walked into the room and kicked the door closed behind her, catching a demon merc by the neck as he charged her. Slowly she lifted his body from the floor, tilting her head from side to side.

"You humans turn the *funniest* shade of blue," she told him as both man and demon struggled.

The demon screamed in the man's mind.

She squeezed her hand tighter until the popping of bones in the merc's neck was audible, then his body went limp and the air left his lungs. She dropped him to the floor and rubbed her palms together.

"Who's next?"

Pandora left the room and headed for the ballroom at the end of the hall, where she could smell more nasty little demons inside.

As she walked in one of the demons lunged and jabbed a knife into her side, then slowly backed up a look of victory on his face. She yawned as she pulled the knife from her side and the merc stared at the wound as it quickly closed, leaving no marks behind.

"That wasn't very nice," she told him as she grabbed him by the neck and jammed his knife into his abdomen.

His eyes went wide and she smiled as she pulled the knife up through his belly. He groaned once before going limp and falling to the floor. She looked at the blood on her hand and grimaced, wiping it on Katie's now-stretched-out shirt.

Three more mercs came out from the back of the room, two holding swords and the other a knife. Their eyes glowed red.

Pandora sighed and pulled the two halves of Katie's quarterstaff from the holsters on her legs.

"How about this?" Pandora told them, stepping forward and looking each one in the eyes. "I'll make it fair. I won't even put the blades out."

Pandora gripped the wooden poles tightly in her hands and flipped herself into the air, spinning her body so that her legs kicked outward. She caught the first merc in the head, almost knocking it off his shoulders. The other two watched as he dropped, dead before his face hit the cold tile.

His knife bounced across the floor and Pandora shook her head.

"Holy shit, Burt!" The middle guy coughed before looking back up at Pandora.

He failed to realize that his demon was trying to hide.

Pandora smirked. "You shouldn't bring a knife to a... Well, really you should have just run."

She whipped her body around again, striking the second merc in the neck and knocking him to his knees.

She handed him her poles, and in his messed-up state he just accepted them without question.

"Here, hold these," she said grabbing his head and twisting hard. The snap of his neck was loud in the quiet of the room. "Thank you."

She picked the poles up off the ground and clicked the button, watching the shiny knives sprang from the ends.

The last merc narrowed his eyes and squatted with his sword in front of him. His demon wasn't trying to hide. It figured the best chance was fighting.

"Bring it, bitch." He spat to the side. "I'll ream your ass with your own poles."

"Kinky!" Pandora laughed. "I might like it. Saves me the worry of you using your pencil dick." She ran toward him and jumped over his outstretched hand and sword to land behind him. The merc pivoted, bringing his sword with him in an arc and barely missing her stomach.

"You almost tore my shirt," she growled.

She swung the pole, clipping his sword, and they fought back and forth as if they were dueling. After about thirty seconds Pandora grew tired of the game and swiped the knives low, cutting the merc across the abdomen. He groaned and dropped his sword, grabbing his stomach instead.

"At least you don't have a headache," she said as he looked up at her pleadingly.

She laid down one of her poles and picked up his sword, then shrugged and slammed the blade into his neck, severing his head. As it rolled across the floor she tossed the sword to the side and picked up her staff, then put the two pieces back into their holsters.

As she looked up and down the hall six more mercs made a break for it, sprinting out the front door into the courtyard. They were met with gunfire and returned fire into the tree line, unable to see exactly where the shots were coming from.

The mercs were firing randomly, but everyone's chances suck at the best of times when lead flies. A bullet struck one of the soldiers next to Ambrose in the head, killing him instantly.

Ambrose growled and stepped forward, firing his weapon over and over. One of the mercs went down, shot in the leg. Ambrose strode over to him and shot him in the forehead.

Another shot rang out and a second went down, dead before he hit the ground. Ambrose spun at the sound of a loud crackle.

He shielded his eyes as lights flashed and sparked and the four remaining mercs disappeared into thin air.

Moloch paced the floor, growling loudly, watching the fight through his magical third eye. The bitch demon was marching through the hotel and taking down man after man. He recognized her right away, and there was nothing he could do to stop her.

He closed his eyes and sent a message to Trenton, who was one of the remaining six.

"Go to the courtyard now! I'll get you out," he commanded.

Trenton nodded and pulled the other mercs toward the door. They sprinted into the courtyard, where they were met with gunfire. Moloch rubbed his hands together and put them out in front of him, creating a portal in the court-yard. When two of his soldiers went down, Trenton grabbed the remaining three and tossed them head-first into the portal. He growled angrily, wanting to turn back and fight them, but knowing that he would lose. There were much bigger battles to be won in the future.

He glanced at the window in the hotel and the demon bitch was looking back at him. She smiled and waved patronizingly.

He turned and dove into the portal and it slammed shut behind him.

She had won this time, but next time he would make sure she wasn't so lucky. He had lost all but three of his men, and he was sure Moloch would not be pleased.

Where that demon had come from and how she had taken over a body like that he had no idea, but he did know that her face was forever burned into his memory.

One day when she was least expecting it, he would find her and sever that pretty little head from her body.

She was obviously powerful, but what he couldn't figure out was why she was fighting for the wrong side.

If she was that strong, she could have easily taken over her human and demolished those troops.

But she hadn't.

Instead she used her power to kill her own, smiling into their faces as they took their last breaths. She was a traitor, and he knew exactly what the demons did to traitors.

This loss would not go unavenged.

———

Korbin stood there gaping, actually listening to the battle radios at the base. The hacker had cracked their system and found the frequency they were broadcasting on.

Ops groups used specially-equipped comms that scrambled the signals so they couldn't be tapped, but somehow, some way, Timothy had managed to tap into the band and was playing it for the whole team.

Korbin had been shocked by Timothy's talent, and he was going to work like hell to keep the man.

There was a ton of screaming coming from inside of the hotel, sometimes recognizable, other times not.

Stephanie clung to Korbin's arm with a worried look on her face. Calvin stood next to Eric listening intently, almost jealous that he hadn't been able to go out there with them. They hadn't been on a call in a while, and all of them were starting to ache for battle.

Another scream rang out and Stephanie shook her head. "Nope, that doesn't sound like Katie."

"Or Damian," Korbin added.

"Another one bites the dust," Calvin exclaimed excitedly. "They are kicking some major demon-merc *ass* right now."

Suddenly a maniacal laugh echoed across the comm, quieting everyone in the room. Calvin looked at the others, wondering if they had recognized that laugh. It seemed he was the only one, but he wasn't about to say a thing—not with Korbin being so far in the dark with Katie's abilities.

"Oh shit," Eric said. "That isn't Katie's voice either."

"Interesting," Korbin remarked, turning up the volume.

The team counted the deaths as they occurred over the comm. After the sixth one, though, everything got quiet for several moments.

Suddenly there was a barrage of gunfire and no one could figure out what the hell was going on. They waited with bated breath, trying to figure out who was shooting and who was being shot.

After two more shots the comm screeched and wailed, and there was a loud bang in the background. Everyone covered their ears until the noises stopped and all that was left was some static.

"What happened?" Eric asked.

Timothy turned the knobs and stared at the screen, then turned to Korbin and shook his head. "That's strange," he said.

"What?" Korbin asked worriedly.

"There must have been a huge energy blast. Not a bomb, but something from fuck-all-if-I-know," he said. "It must have knocked out the comms. I have to be honest: I've never seen anything like that spike in my life."

"Let's just hope that everyone else is okay," Korbin said, hugging Stephanie tightly to his side. "Katie and Damian are professionals, and it would take a lot more than a little energy to knock them off their feet."

A little *energy?* Timothy thought. *What is major energy?*

Korbin sounded sure on the outside, but he didn't know what to expect.

"Are you all right?" Damian called as he ran into the ballroom.

"Right as rain," Pandora called back, looking around. "But I'm afraid my clock has struck midnight." She looked Damian in the eyes. "Take care of Katie. I'm sure we will talk soon."

"Pandora!" Damian grabbed her arm. "Thank you."

"No problem, priesty." She winked. "Imagine that—a priesty and a demon being best buds."

Damian smiled as Pandora closed her eyes and a big surge of energy surrounded her body.

The change from Pandora back to Katie wasn't quite as freaky as the one that had brought Pandora out.

Instead, Katie's body floated into the air and basked in the bright light, and then carefully and slowly descended.

Damian waited for all of the energy to dissipate before running to Katie's side.

He looked down at her familiar face; everything was

back to the way it should be. Damian sighed in relief and knelt next to her as she opened her eyes and slowly sat up.

"Oh, my head," she cried, grabbing her forehead. "Did we get them?"

"You don't remember any of it?" Damian asked.

"No." Katie sighed. "I don't remember anything after ducking into that old woodshed out front. What happened when Pandora took over?"

"You were gone," Damian told her. "Your whole body was different, your face was different, and your voice wasn't the same. You were completely a different person. Pandora took over, but it wasn't like when other demons take over and practically shred the human they are in. She morphed into herself with you sleeping—or something close to it—on the inside."

"Really?" she exclaimed, looking down at her now-baggy top. "Man, her tits stretched out my shirt."

Sorry, Pandora whispered.

Pandora, are you okay?

A little weak, she admitted. *But okay.*

Damian watched Katie's face, noticing that she had tranced out. It was obvious that she was talking to Pandora.

Damian didn't want to interrupt, so he waited impatiently for her to be done. He wanted to know how she felt, and how the whole thing had affected both of them.

Katie looked great. Rosy cheeks, bright eyes—almost like she had woken up from a really good nap.

"Is she okay?" Damian asked, finally too worried to hold back.

"Yeah," Katie answered. "She says she's weak, but that's it."

"She really saved a lot of lives today." Damian shrugged. "She is one hell of a fighter."

Likewise, bestie, Pandora replied.

"She said 'Likewise, bestie.'" Katie raised an eyebrow. "You've replaced me already?"

"No." Damian laughed. "She was just really great, that's all. She killed six of the demon mercs inside the hotel. You killed two in the woods, and the soldiers took down two more."

"Nice." Katie smiled. "What about the other four?"

"They disappeared into a portal of some kind," Damian replied. "We don't really know what happened with that. All we know is that they are gone. *Pissed*, but gone."

"Well, I'm glad that Pandora was here. Those demon mercs are a pain in the ass." Katie cricked her neck after Damian helped her to her feet.

"I want to ask you something," Damian began carefully. "Allowing your demon to take you over like that takes a lot of trust. She could have run off with your body in two seconds. You trust her that much?"

"Of course I trust her!" Katie exclaimed. "I wouldn't have okayed this if I didn't. I trust her with my *life*. Pandora is my sister. My friend, even; one of the very few people who have been there for me from the beginning."

"She's a *demon*," Damian replied, looking at Katie curiously. "She is a body-snatching human-eating demon."

Katie pursed her lips and ran her hand over Damian's cheek. She understood his concerns; she did. She even understood his hatred toward the whole demon race, but Pandora was different. Finally she cracked a smile.

"Damian," she whispered. "Aren't we *all* a little bit demon?"

———

General Brushwood looked down at the hotel as the chopper flew over, seeing the soldiers standing out in the courtyard.

There was a row of stretchers with white sheets covering the deceased.

The first in the line of bodies stood out—the one military casualty that they had taken. The soldiers had lowered the American flag that still flew from the hotel's flagpole and draped it carefully over the soldier's body.

The general felt a knot in his stomach. He hated to see his men perish at the hands of such evil.

One dead soldier was one too many, and that went for their allies as well as civilians.

The helicopter lowered to the ground and Colonel Ambrose ran up and opened the door, then stepped to the side and saluted the general. He returned the salute and the two men ducked away from the chopper. They walked down the side of the hill and into the courtyard where the remaining soldiers stood at attention.

"At ease," the general ordered. "It is I who should be standing at attention for you. You held the line against one of the greatest threats to mankind that we have found on this Earth. You singlehandedly took out eight of the fourteen demon mercs who were here today. That is something to be extremely proud of."

"Sir, if I may?" the colonel asked. "We have to give credit where credit is due. Katie took out eight of the ten dead demon mercs tonight."

"But where would we have been without you there backing us up?" Katie asked in return, joining the colonel and the general.

"Katie!" The general smiled as he shook her hand. "Are you all right?"

"I'm fine, although flipping roles from businesswoman to demon hunter *is* a bit exhausting," she replied. Damian chuckled in the background.

"Thank you for your service." The colonel saluted Katie.

She looked at the soldiers who were listening in and they all bounced to attention and saluted her as well, warming her heart. She knew exactly how special that was, and she was glad she had been there to save some lives.

They're saluting you, Pandora, Katie said, smiling to the men.

Pandora sniffled. *Mmmhmm.*

Are you getting emotional?

No, she growled. *I have demon-merc cooties in my eye, that's all.*

Oh, okay. Katie snickered.

After the moment had passed Katie moved back and stood next to Damian. He put his arm around her shoulders and squeezed her tightly as they listened to the general address his troops.

While it was a celebration, it was nowhere near being the end of the story.

"We have recently received a bit more information from an FBI effort that has been in the works," Brushwood told them. "It seems likely that there will soon be about a hundred and twenty demon mercs in this group. We don't know how many separate groups there will be, if any; that's all we have. From what I've been told, one of those bodies over there is one of the leaders of the group. Now, we aren't sure if he was the top man, but everyone counts. Research is getting better every day, especially with the addition of a new IT tech at the Korbin's Killers' base. He has jumped on the bandwagon and already made his mark. I don't want anyone to be down after today. It's true, we lost another one of our men and that is tragic in many ways, but we are going to bag these assholes. That is a promise that I will stand here and make to you today. There will be no more surprises, no more anger, and no more crossing lines. We will be ready for them if it's the *last* thing I ever do."

The alarm blared loudly echoing through the bus.

Brock groaned and leaned over to silence it, knocking an empty bottle of Jack onto the floor before pounding his hand on the button. He laid back down and stretched his arms over his head, yawning.

He opened his eyes, and next to him were three stark-naked busty blondes sprawled across the bed. He smiled and rubbed his hand down the closest one's back.

She moaned slightly and opened her eyes, blinking at Brock.

"I thought it was a dream." She yawned as she looked at the other two girls.

"It *was* a dream," he agreed, and kissed her. "But dreams come true."

The other girls began to stir, climbing up the bed and wrapping themselves around him. All three started to kiss his skin, forcing him to take a deep breath and put his arms in the air. Unfortunately, he didn't have the time for another go, nor did he really think he had the energy.

Those three were wild, and he had been the only one drinking the night before.

He sighed. "Ladies, as much as I would love to stay in bed with you, I mustn't."

"Awwww," all three groaned in unison, giving him pouty lips.

He pulled himself from the bed and put on his robe, then turned around and laughed. "Don't give me those faces. I have to hit the road. I'm headed home for a little vacation with my family."

"When will you be back in Virginia?" one of them asked, sitting up and pulling her fingers through her wild hair.

Brock shrugged. "I don't know," he answered as truthfully as he could. When the truth works, use it. "I'm sure we will come through here again on tour. When we do, I want to see all three of you here waiting for me."

One of the other girls chuckled. "You better believe it."

All three of them got up and searched the room for their clothes, giggling as they traded pieces back and forth until they found almost full outfits. Brock leaned into the closet and grabbed three band t-shirts and tossed one to each. They smiled and pulled them on, bearing the marks of sin all too well.

"Thank you," the three said in unison.

"Now come here and give me a kiss on my cheek before you leave," he demanded, pointing to his cheek.

One by one the girls leaned in and gave him a long sensual kiss on the cheek, and he chuckled as he followed them out of the back room and through the bus to the door. His bandmates were all awake and drank coffee while they watched the three hotties leave.

He waved as the girls walked away, then shut the door and came back to the main area.

"I don't know how you do it!" his drummer exclaimed. "Dude, you have at least three women almost every night. I seriously feel drained from just *one* of those nympho groupies."

"That's because you're an old man." Brock laughed and ruffled the drummer's hair.

"I am all of three years older than you." He scoffed. "I just don't have the magic spark you seem to have."

"Yeah, and you must have had extra last night because I think they heard those women moaning in Jersey," his bassist joked. "It turned on my girl a bit, so I can't complain."

"Annnnd... *You're welcome.*" Brock smiled and went to the closet, pulling out a somewhat clean pair of jeans and a t-shirt.

He pulled on his clothes and tossed the robe into the back room before going to the table to get a cup of the coffee that had been delivered earlier that morning.

He stretched his back, already feeling ten times better than he had when he'd first woken up.

His phone buzzed and he saw that his car was there and ready to take him to the airport.

He grabbed the suitcase he'd packed the night before and looked at the guys.

"So, you taking that game back to your hometown?" His guitarist laughed.

"Nah." He shrugged. "I think I got everything I need."

He pulled his sunglasses down as he stepped out into the sun to hide the tinge of red in his eyes.

FINIS

AUTHOR NOTES - MICHAEL ANDERLE

WRITTEN MAY 17, 2018

First, THANK YOU for taking this ride with us for a group of stories that can be a bit hard to sell.

Then you tried to tell your spouses and friends just *why* it's so damned fun! (Damned...hehehe.)

I apologize that some of them won't understand, and I really appreciate your efforts to tell them. It is hard to actually constrain Katie / Pandora to a few short words...

Which means *I* have to try it now.

College Woman Not Seeking Live-In Demon, Fails Miserably —Much Shit Happens.

Ok...maybe not that one.

Demon political shit runs right over nice, caring Katie, who was sacrificed at the wrong place and at the wrong time.

Huh...not exactly.

Female Demon desires a little R & R from the machinations down in Hell. Looking for an unwilling vessel and donuts.

Well, shoot...Pandora didn't know about donuts at that time.

Military Action story when eons-old female demon with no inhibitions takes up residence inside obstinate college-age woman who is just fine with her bra size. Much ass-kicking occurs.

That is perhaps a little closer to the truth.

The real answer is a lot longer, I think. As an indie author, we don't have 'people' to do our blurbs. For the most part we do them ourselves, and since we are so close to them, the challenge is stepping back and getting to the heart of what these stories are about.

I think of them as "tough times call for tough measures and whether you like the new reality (when you have a demon) or not doesn't matter. It's time to buck up (and buckle up) and shut up."

You MUST choose one of three options.

—OTHER NEWS

We are rapidly coming to the end of the first series, Protected by the Damned. "Things" are going to happen which will propagate (read 'explode') the reality to the rest of the world, and then we will move Katie and Pandora into a new series titled "War of the Damned."

I won't ruin anything. I just wanted to let those of you asking know that YES, Katie and Pandora have another series after Book 08, *For Whom the Bell Tolls*, coming out June 1, 2018.

For those in the Facebook group, THANK YOU for all of your stories, your jokes and your hijinks. You keep me in stitches and offer up very interesting suggestions and comments.

In book 8, we will have a special redshirt walk-on event

for one of our fans from the group. I hope he enjoys dying spectacularly ;-)

Ad Aeternitatem,

Michael Todd Anderle

PANDORA'S TURN

All right, you little miscreants, just because The Chubby Author ™ was all nice and shit above, don't expect the same from me. I'm onto you!

I have visited the dreams of a few of you. For those who were very naughty...that was fun! No, seriously, you *pervs*.

For those who received *ugly* dreams, no comment. I hope you mend your ways and take appropriate action (you know what I'm talking about).

For the young woman who asked about the boob job? Sorry, I'm stuck in this body for the moment. I still have my way with her, but it just takes a lot longer.

Ok, I'm told I have to go eat some donuts, so ta-ta, you little miscreants! See you in the next book!

Pandora

AUTHOR NOTES - LAURIE STARKEY

WRITTEN

Well hello! Thanks for stopping by to read my author note. I appreciate that big time. I never wrong author notes, because honestly – my life is crazy as hell and boring outside of the craze. Not quite sure that made sense, but we're going with it.

Mike talked me into author notes. Blame him if this blows dog balls.

Speaking of Mike... I just got back from 21 days on the road, a few of those spent with him. We worked through some really cool ideas for Damned spin-offs (< ---- see what I did there? LOL). I'll let him fill you in on that goodness, but I am 100% stoked about the ideas we bubbled up together.

Outside of the all of the great writing goodies, we've been looking for a house up in the hill country near New Braunfels. I think we finally found one. Now it's time to beg the banker man for a few dollars to buy the damn thing.

Funny – no matter how old you are or what dollar amount you have in the bank, something about having to borrow money (at least for me) feels like I'm dick-broke, 16 and ready to get rejected. It's rather humbling. I'm thinking renting might be a better option – at least for my freaking pride.

My team is throat deep over here (that's horrible sounding from a romance writer – forgive me in advance) in 7sons goodies. Our first vamp book is through editing and the final touches are making their way on the file. I have a short excerpt for you below, but before I hand that over – once again – thank you so much. I appreciate you checking out mine and Mike's project. It's a blessing to work with him, but it's an honor to write for you.

Excerpt from Bad Moon Rising, Seven Sons:

Turning into a narrow alley, the darkness grew thicker around her, and the cold bit just that touch deeper and sharper with every step. The dull, brown brick Georgian buildings pressed heavily in, creating only an arrowhead of inky, velvet sky overhead. Most of the factories looked abandoned after the working day was done, windows grimy behind heavy iron bars. Litter from the neighboring fast food stores gathered in the gutters, blown in from vacant construction sites gazetted for industry.

London had never seemed so dismal.

Not that she was aware of it or even felt it; there were other things occupying her mind. It had been a long and difficult day, and pervasive memories of vivid faces continued to plague her still. There remained an indescribable loneliness.

Somewhere in the distance, Big Ben began to strike the hour.

With each heavy chime, she could feel the moment fragmenting, she could feel the stillness of time falling.

When will it stop? Aislinn wondered, restlessly.

She felt an echo of her former self. Her past faded behind the city blocks. Her future stretched before her in that moment, thin and insubstantial, down the darkened street.

*

The man paused in the shadows. Sneaking a quick glance across at the young girl he was following, he was surprised to find that she wasn't showing any signs of being affected by, or even aware of, their miserable surroundings. In fact, she seemed particularly immune to almost everything around her, except the pealing echoes from Big Ben.

His fingers twitched nervously around the switchblade in his hand as if anticipating the moment when he would feel it slice through her warm flesh. But not before he'd had some fun with her first. Pretty young things like the pale, blonde-haired girl before him didn't venture into this part of London-town often. He took a moment to let his eyes roam up her body.

Fuck. Who was he kidding?

Pretty young things almost never came to his part of town, unless they were looking to buy some meth or coke or that new drug he'd been hearing a lot about; Black Mambo or Black Magic or whatever it was called. Maybe that was why she was here. Hoping to score. Well, so was he. And he'd lucked in. He usually had to go find them.

He watched her possessively, tension in every muscle. His fleshy, pock-marked face broke into a lascivious smile. He liked the way she moved. Graceful. Like a dancer. Her platinum-

blonde hair fell down her back to her waist, a waterfall of harnessed moonlight. He could feel his heart beat wildly; so loud and fast it pounded against his rib cage, thrumming in his ears, momentarily drowning out her footsteps.

Again, his hand twitched, feeling the familiar weight of the blade.

His tongue poked out between suddenly dry lips.

Delicious.

*

She stopped at a corner beneath the awning of an empty curiosity shop, an aged sign in the grime-streaked storefront window advertised that it was up for lease. Hesitating briefly, she knew better than to linger on darkened city street corners, but she knew something wasn't right. An instinct honed back at the beginning of duration for all living creatures. A prickling sensation along the back of her neck.

Like the hunter and the hunted, the predator and the prey, she sensed that something – someone – was following her.

The streetlamps flickered up and down the laneway as if by a surge of her own adrenaline, but the muted yellow glow they emitted wasn't enough to keep the darkness at bay.

With an anxious thrill bordering on agony, Aislinn set off down the grim alleyway, the rain beginning to fall softly with the onset of another restless night. Each darkened doorway, boarded up window, fluttering streetlamp that she walked past became a familiar blur of insidious intent.

Close! He's close! Aislinn thought, experiencing a strange sense of déjà vu.

She fixed eyes the colour of cornflowers upon the alleyway ahead, picking up her pace as she saw his shadow under the streetlights slide along the granite setts, matching her pace.

Aislinn felt herself tense, readying herself for the attack. The cold air gusted and made her platinum-blonde hair and long leather coat flap violently about her. The broken blinds and chimney pots were filled with the blustering wind, whistling between gaps in the narrow alley. But she barely noticed.

Shhh. Aislinn. Calm down.

He's close.

He's close now.

She tried not to look over her shoulder. She could have easily confirmed that he was following her, but she deliberately chose not to. Instead, she quickened her pace. That ancient voice that warned her to be cautious spoke up; shouting in her ear like the frosty draughts of winter wind which infiltrated the alleyway's hollow nooks and crannies, slipping furtively under window-panes and doors, and between the cracks and gaps in brick and plasterwork.

Don't let him know you're aware of him. Just keep going. Keep walking. Careful now, Aislinn.

*

He continued to dog the girl's footsteps. She was making it easy for him, even with her quickened pace. Her head was bowed low, shoulders hunched, hands thrust into her coat pockets to protect herself from the increasing wind and rain.

She seemed anxious. This slip of a girl with the moonlight hair who was so young-looking, though most probably in her early twenties. This pretty, young thing whom he would make sob in the pitch black.

He hoped she would scream. He liked it when they screamed. He was going to take good care of her.

It was easy.

He'd done it before. Twice. And each time he felt stronger, more confident, more adept.

The gloomy alley was completely empty, except for the rain and the rats and himself and the girl. Even the rats were scampering for cover.

Silly girl.

Anyone who needed a hit that badly deserved what was coming to them. Or maybe she was buying drugs to go clubbing later with her foolish friends. It was Friday night and the nightclubs and bars nearby were always jampacked with fresh meat.

But they weren't here with her now. Instead, she was alone.

It seemed like they were the only two people left on earth. He relished the thought. And soon there would only be one.

The tension in his shoulders began to fade as he readied himself for the kill. She wasn't going anywhere.

"Hey, girly. You lost?" he asked, approaching her from behind. His words carried towards her on the wind.

As if startled, like a jittery colt, she whirled around to face him before he reached her.

Flawless pale skin, a pixie-like face, and fathomless dark eyes.

It was the eyes that made him pause, gripping his blade even more tightly. They gave him the creeps. Either there was something so deeply buried, he wouldn't find it unless she wanted him to or — or he could see nothing behind the girl's eyes.

"No. I'm not lost. Are you?" she said. Her voice was flat, emotionless. Like her eyes.

A sickness roiled in the center of his stomach.

She was reaching for him with her eyes. It was like she was holding him back from tumbling over the edge of eternity. And she would catch him before he fell.

The man experienced one shivering moment of silence, frozen into immobility, until a damp gust of icy winter wind bringing stinging rain blew into his eyes, making him blink and squint in shocked reaction as he gazed through wet lashes upon the most horrifying sight he would ever see.

She smiled.

It didn't reach her eyes.

There was nothing human in her eyes. Only a deadly cold, pure rage. Razor-sharp incisors broke through her gums, snapping down in a matter of seconds into place. They weren't like any teeth he'd ever seen before. Not on humans nor animals. They were like polished ivory. Protruding slightly from her mouth, wickedly strong and tapered.

She reached across and took the switchblade easily from his nerveless hand, disarming him. He didn't even try to put up a fight or resist her. He couldn't.

He wanted to grab it back. He wanted to pull away, even though she wasn't even touching him. He wanted to run. But, somehow, he couldn't gain control of his responses. He couldn't gain control of himself.

Paralyzed, all he could do was watch as she brought the blade up to his neck and placed the sharpened tip against his pulsing throat. It drew blood. He could feel it. Even with the rain splattering him in the face, he felt his heated blood trickling down his skin.

Her thin nostrils flared in response, as if breathing in his scent.

He couldn't scream. He couldn't speak. He couldn't even breathe.

Her eyes were obsidian pools that made all the blood drain from his head. His heart fluttered like a trapped bird inside his ribcage. Her look was knowing. She would set it free.

"I know what you were thinking," she whispered, her voice now sweetly intoxicating and sultry. "You were wondering, what's a nice girl like me doing in a place like this?"

He released the smallest whimper as she leaned into him and licked his neck, right over the quivering pulse.

"Mmmm—" She licked her lips like the cat with the canary, savoring the moment when he finally realized that all along she had been the predator and he was the prey. She could see it in his darting eyes. The fear. Her power. The beauty of it. "Don't worry. I'm going to take good care of you."

It was easy.

Delicious.

*

"Dammit, Aislinn. You're late."

"I stopped off for a bite to eat before work." Aislinn tossed off a sassy reply over her shoulder as she hung her leather coat in the back office, grabbing a tablet from the counter to check the club's inventory list. "Besides, it's Friday night. Hump night. It'll only be the regulars; the rest will be trolling the Street Buffet."

Caleb grunted. He would have liked nothing more than to reprimand her, but he refrained. Not only would Aislinn not have welcomed it – welcomed it? Vlad's balls! She would have performed root canal treatment on him without batting an eyelash – but she was already too anaemic as it was, pushing the feeding time often to the third day, almost to the last minute, and the limits of any normal vampire's endurance.

Watching her organise the Nocturne's weekly stocktake, she looked as fragile as a will-o'-the-wisp, a dandelion that would blow away in the first strong wind.

But looks could be deceiving.

The burly bartender ran one large hand over his bald head, as if massaging a chronic headache. Muscles bulged from his beefy biceps, the intricate tattoos snaking and rippling along his bronzed skin as if alive. His left arm sported the motto, "Fortis Fortuna Adiuvat"; his right, "Fortes Fortuna Iuvat", proclaiming his hardcore military background. But even with all his military training and many kills, the slight figure of the girl in front of him made him feel extremely nervous and protective in equal measure.

She was the last of The Twelve turned by Kayne himself; the father of them all. Yet the only female. Why Kayne chose her as his Twelfth Disciple was anybody's guess. She was the most troublesome, defiant, wilful baggage around. And a pain in the ass to mentor.

Perhaps that was why Kayne had abandoned her to the care of Julius and the London Coven. A mistake, in his opinion. Two of Kayne's direct descendants under the one roof made for World War V.

"Chillax, old man. Why don't you have a drink?" Aislinn teased, sensing his discord, as she tossed her platinum locks back over her shoulder and moved to stand behind the bar.

"Maybe I will. What's our stock like?" was his gruff reply.

Aislinn rolled her eyes. Honestly, in all the time she'd known him, Caleb still couldn't – or wouldn't – cast aside his rigidity. He was a stickler for the rules. Must have been his time spent in the army – make that armies; he liked to re-enlist every hundred years or so for the fun of it. But despite sharing ownership of the Nocturne with her, he would never take from his own merchandise. It was always rations and supplies, then surplus.

"All good. Don't get your fangs in a furrow," she replied, passing him the tablet for his inspection. "We're receiving the new delivery from the Blood Bank tomorrow, not tonight. Nikolaus was very apologetic when he called. He's handling it personally. We're the first on his route – well, after Styx."

"Of course, we are. Nikolaus has the hots for you. He wants to make the beast with two backs," Caleb mocked, hoping to get a rise out of her. Aislinn didn't even bother to respond; she'd heard it all before.

To be continued...

Slave to many stories,

Laurie Starkey

BOOKS BY MICHAEL TODD

PROTECTED BY THE DAMNED
Torn Asunder (01)
Killing Is My Business (02)
And Business Is Good (03)
Sit Down, Shut Up, And Pull The Trigger (04)
Welcome To The Jungle (05)
Metal Up Your Ass (06)
Dirty Deeds Done Dirt Cheap (07)

(04) - Unlawful Passage (05) - Darkness Rises (06) - The Gods Beneath (07) - Reborn (08)

THE HIDDEN MAGIC CHRONICLES
with Justin Sloan

Shades of Light (01) - Shades of Dark (02) - Shades of Glory (03) - Shades of Justice (04)

STORMS OF MAGIC
with PT Hylton

Storm Raiders (01) - Storm Callers (02) - Storm Breakers (03) - Storm Warrior (04)

TALES OF THE FEISTY DRUID
with Candy Crum

The Arcadian Druid (01) - The Undying Illusionist (02) - The Frozen Wasteland (03) - The Deceiver (04) - The Lost (05) - The Damned (06) - Into The Maelstrom (07)

PATH OF HEROES
with Brandon Barr

Rogue Mage (01)

A NEW DAWN
with Amy Hopkins

Dawn of Destiny (01) - Dawn of Darkness (02) - Dawn of Deliverance (03) - Dawn of Days (04) - Broken Skies (05) - Broken Bones (06)

TALES OF THE WELLSPRING KNIGHT

with P.J. Cherubino

Knight's Creed (01) - Knight's Struggle (02) - Knight's Justice (03)

~THE AGE OF MADNESS~

LIVE FREE OR DIE

with Haley Lawson

Unleashing Madness (01)

~THE AGE OF EXPANSION~

THE ASCENSION MYTH

*with Ell Leigh Clarke *

Awakened (01) - Activated (02) - Called (03) - Sanctioned (04) -
Rebirth (05) - Retribution (06) - Cloaked (07) - Bourne (08) -
Committed (09) - Subversion (10)

CONFESSIONS OF A SPACE ANTHROPOLOGIST

with Ell Leigh Clarke

Giles Kurns: Rogue Operator (01) - Giles Kurns: Rogue Instigator
(02)

THE UPRISE SAGA

*with Amy Duboff *

Covert Talents (01) - Endless Advance (02) - Veiled Designs (03) -
Dark Rivals (04)

BAD COMPANY
with Craig Martelle

The Bad Company (01) - Blockade (02) - Price of Freedom (03) - Liberation (04)

THE GHOST SQUADRON
with Sarah Noffke and J.N. Chaney

Formation (01) - Exploration (02) - Evolution (03) - Degeneration (04) - Impersonation (05) - Recollection (06) - Preservation (07)

VALERIE'S ELITES
with Justin Sloan and PT Hylton

Valerie's Elites (01) - Death Defied (02) - Prime Enforcer (03) - Justice Earned

SHADOW VANGUARD
with Tom Dublin

Gravity Storm (01)

ETHERIC ADVENTURES: ANNE AND JINX
with S.R. Russell

Etheric Recruit (01) - Etheric Researcher (02)

Other Books
with Craig Martelle & Justin Sloan

Gateway to the Universe

SHORT STORIES

The Lone Ranger Returns (Pew!Pew!)

You Don't Touch John's Cousin: Frank Kurns Stories of the UnknownWorld 01 (7.5)

Bitch's Night Out: Frank Kurns Stories of the UnknownWorld 02 (9.5)

with Natalie Grey

Bellatrix: Frank Kurns Stories of the Unknownworld 03 (13.25)

Challenges: Frank Kurns Stories of the Unknownworld 04

AudioBooks

Available at Audible.com and iTunes

www.ingramcontent.com/pod-product-compliance
Lightning Source LLC
Chambersburg PA
CBHW050228110726
47898CB00007B/2070